Irish Mist

Kris J. Rennie

Irish Mist

Copyright © 2020 by Kris J. Rennie
All rights reserved.

Cover painting by Lydia Rennie

Image page 154 Copyright © 2020 by Susan McEwen

Image page 186 Copyright © 2020 by Betsy Feinberg

Image page 191 used under the terms of the
GNU Free Documentation License

No part of this book may be reproduced in any form or by any electronic or mechanical means including information storage and retrieval systems, without permission in writing from the publisher.

This is a work of fiction. Names, characters, businesses, places, events, locales, and incidents are either the products of the author's imagination or used in a fictitious manner. Any resemblance to actual persons, living or dead, or actual events is purely coincidental.

Printed in the United States of America

First Printing August 2020

ISBN 978-1-64970-614-0 Paperback

Published by: Book Services
                www.BookServices.us

Contents

Dedication v

1. The Well 1
2. The Boy on the Rock 85
3. The Trees that Grow Old 107
4. The Whistle on the Wind 147
5. The Salt of the Earth 169

Epilogue 191

About the Author 193

Map of Canada 194

Irish Mist

Dedication

To my birth mother, Alice, who left her
muse for me to find,
in the ashes beside her headstone.

Irish Mist

Chapter 1
The Well

#1 Colleen

Papa sent me out to fetch water from the well. I knew what that meant. He wanted to be alone with Mama. He knew that a layer of ice would have formed on the surface of the water overnight, with the cold weather being what it was. I would have to get a heavy weight and tie a cord to it in order to break through the ice. Only then could I lower the bucket and fill it with water. That all would take quite a while. It would've been a different story if it had been Mama that had asked me to get the water. She was all practical in her thinking, and she would have given me the brick from the hearth and the piece of rope that was needed to get the job done. That way she would have had the water a lot faster, if she had really wanted it.

Either way, I needed to put on boots and a coat. My mittens hung by the stove, still not dry from my

last venture out for wood. It had been snowing for days. The cold north wind was howling something fierce, and the cracks around the windows let in puffs of snow with each gust. Would winter ever end? I was tired of wearing so many clothes. I longed for the days when I could go to the lake with my friends and swing on a rope into the cool depths. We would catch frogs and Mama would cook them up. We would run through the meadows and collect wildflowers to decorate the table. Clean laundry would dry in the warm breezes, rather than freezing, board-stiff, damp, and cold when it was brought inside. It was embarrassing to have my underclothes on display by the fire.

Chapter 1 - The Well

As I pulled on my damp mittens and shoved my girl-feet into my brother's boots, I grumbled to myself. "Why do I have to go?" I answered my own question, muttering, "Because your brothers aren't here now, are they?" They had left town six months past, at the beginning of summer. The two of them had packed up all the belongings they could fit into the back of Andy's Honda and left the small farm for the big city, or what they considered to be a big city. Anywhere was bigger than— well, *here*.

Here was our town, Back of Beyond, Saskatchewan, population 602. We had a post office, a gas station, the farmers' co-op, and a barbershop/hair salon next to the municipal office. The church occupied the largest piece of property at the start of the main street. Its tall-to-the-sky bell tower and stern, grey brick exterior sent a clear message to any folk that came into town. This was a God-fearing community. The schoolroom was in the basement of the church; it smelled musty and the fluorescent lighting flickered, giving me a sick feeling. There was a rumour that Sybil Bisbee was running a liquor business from the back porch of her house. She lived a block behind Main Street. It seemed to me that there was a lot of back and forth going on, on Back Street.

I searched around for a stone or piece of discarded brick that would be small enough for me to pry from the frozen dirt but heavy enough to break the ice. I found the rope that I needed to keep the weight from free-falling to the bottom of the well. It, too, was firmly frozen to the ground. The dogs followed me,

3

doing their running game and playing with each other all the while. They didn't care that it was cold, or that I was annoyed by being sent out for water that we didn't need right now, just because Papa and Mama wanted to practise baby-making. Like I didn't know about such things. I was almost 14 now, I'd heard talk. One of the Irwin sisters had found herself in trouble last year. She had been shipped off to the city, where her aunt and uncle lived. At first I thought maybe she had taken something without asking and had been sent away to learn her lesson, but now I knew better. The boys that sat behind me at school had been snickering and talking among themselves, thinking I couldn't hear them. Well, I had heard plenty! I knew about those things. I wasn't going to let anyone convince me to show my knickers. No way. I didn't want to get myself in that kind of trouble.

I finally managed to tie the rope around the bit of brick and dropped it down onto the icy surface of the water. I had to do it a few times before it broke through. I guess Papa would be happy I was taking so long. I leaned over the side of the well. The angle of the plunging bucket had to be just right or the thing would float instead of filling with water. There was something down there. I could see its soft edges under the jagged surface of broken ice. The curling mist came up from the frigid water, wrapping itself around my wool hat, finding the space between my collar and my neck, slipping under my thick sweater and then stopping where my heart beat hard and fast. My mind turned fancy cartwheels trying to sort out what had just happened. Or even if it had happened at all? Must

Chapter 1 - The Well

have been my creative thinking. Mama always said I had my head in the mist, like the Irish colleen I had been named after. My fiery spirit was easily seen; it didn't take a lot of hard looking.

I hauled up the bucket, now filled with fresh water. I coiled the ice-covered rope, leaving the brick still attached this time. I left it beside the well, ready for use. I'd be in trouble if too many rocks and things were dropping into the well.

The dogs had found a groundhog to torment. They played with the poor creature, circling it and barking. If it was out and about, my wish for spring would be granted soon. I knew about groundhogs too. I trudged back through the muddy snow to the house, thinking that my parents' need for privacy must be done by now. It usually didn't take long for them to finish up. I hardly noticed that the deep snow was now turning to mud. I did notice the dripping icicles by the door.

#2 The Hens

I took off my brother's boots and hung my coat on its hook in the small room off the back porch. The fire in the hearth had been stoked and Mama was busy in the kitchen, chopping vegetables that had been stored in the root cellar. She was smiling to herself, as the long-handled knife sliced through the overwintered carrots. "Stew will be ready soon," she announced to no one in particular.

Irish Mist

The hook that held Papa's barn clothes was empty. He had probably gone out to fix the fence around the chicken coop; it needed mending again. We could ill afford to have wild animals and feral dogs getting to the hens and their eggs.

I put the heavy, sloshing bucket down by the sink. The hand pump only worked when the line to the house was clear of ice. "I wish this cold wind would move on. I had to drop that brick three times before I could lower the pail. I hate winter!" I hoped that a bit of whining would save me from going to the well again soon. This last trip had me feeling strange. But as usual, my complaining only got me more chores to do. I would be busy for the rest of the day.

When Papa came in for his dinner, which smelled pretty darn good, his coat was unbuttoned and his wool hat was stuffed into the pocket. I looked up from the sink and the fresh eggs I was washing. "Getting warm out there," he said, as he wiped his brow with his old red handkerchief. "Wind's calmed down; there's hardly a breath of air in that coop! We're going to have to spend the afternoon changing the straw. Smells bad enough to kill a skunk! Colleen, that other stuff will have to wait—this needs doing today. Book reading can wait too." I looked up at him again, that strange feeling wiggling around like butterflies in my belly.

The chicken coop was indeed in a mess. There was mud mixed with the soiled hay bedding. The acrid smell of ammonia from accumulating manure was overpowering. I grabbed the pitchfork and began

Chapter 1 - The Well

removing many months' worth of soggy straw. The hens were not impressed by my intrusive behavior. They flapped about and vocalized their displeasure. The latch to the barnyard dislodged, and a dozen frantic chickens let themselves free of their pen. I dropped the pitchfork in the mud. As I tried in vain to stop their escape, I could hear the sucking noise of defrosting ground coming from my boots. The hens became distracted by the fresh green shoots sprouting up around the fence posts and slowed to pecking speed. Papa was now in his rolled-up shirtsleeves, a frown on his face as he looked into the distance.

The creek that was barely a semi-frozen ribbon of water in winter had grown to a torrent that threatened its banks. The ice crust was gone and as the water rushed forward and down, its path widened and the shape of its curve straightened. The surging flow was headed towards the house. Papa yelled out to me, "Forget the hens! Get the sandbags." This day was surely going from bad to worse. I wished my brothers were here to help.

#3 The Cat

When Papa and I finished up outside, the sun was sending us goodnight kisses. We were done in. Trying to keep up with the sudden warm weather, the rushing creek, and our escaped critters had left us bone weary and scatterbrained. We trudged to the house, hung up our barn clothes and washed the manure and mud from our hands. The big pot on the back of the wood stove was not steaming as it should be, and the water

Irish Mist

was only half warm. Mama always kept hot water at the ready for washing up after supper. She had left us some food on the table. It had gone cold. Where was she?

The house was quiet. The dogs were lying on the porch, their empty bowls waiting to be filled. I could see the day's laundry still on the line, hanging limp in the windless air. As I stood in the kitchen trying to figure things out, Papa went through the narrow hallway towards the back bedroom. He was not a man to give in to panic, but I heard his raised voice calling my mother's name. "Edith! What are you doing there?" I could not make sense of her mumbled reply.

Thinking it was none of my business, I set about feeding myself. When I had finished my plate, I moved to the porch to feed the dogs. The big bowl of water that they shared was empty, and I realized that I would need to get more from the well. As I passed by the sink to get the galvanized pail, I saw the pump faucet dripping. That meant I could save myself a trip outside. It also meant that the ice in the line was melting.

Papa came out to the main room as I was working the hand pump, marvelling that it was producing a steady stream of cold water. "Mama's hit her head on the chest at the end of the bed. She's coming around now. Must have tripped over something. You let the cat in the house again, didn't you? I don't know how many times I've told you. Now look what's happened. Where's your head, Colleen? First you let the chickens get out and now you've let that damn cat in!"

Chapter 1 - The Well

Mama could hardly stand, and she had to be helped into bed. I busied myself finishing up all the chores that she had left undone. The wash was brought in, the dogs were fed, I stoked the stove and brought the water to boil. By the time I got the kitchen cleaned, I thought I would drop to the ground myself. But all that scrubbing did not get rid of the uneasy feeling in my belly.

The next day, Papa called for the doctor to drive out from town. Mama was no better, maybe even worse. Dr. McCall arrived before noon, and the dogs gave him a loud greeting, their tails doing double time. He always brought something in his pocket for them. I had known Dr. McCall since I was born. He had brought me into the world, same as my brothers, in the bedroom of this house. He was a wise man and a kind man. We could trust his decisions. He said Mama had a bad concussion, and she would need to be quiet and rest for at least two weeks. Papa's relief at hearing that his Edith was going to be okay was obvious. He looked at me, his frown returning. "Well, Colleen, you are going to have to look after the women's work for now. I'd best get in touch with those two brothers of yours and get them to come home and help out."

#4 The Dog

On Saturday morning, Mama was resting comfortably in the big four-poster bed. Grampa Timmons had made that bed as a wedding gift for his son, Arthur, and Edith, his new bride. Grampa had carved it out of wood he had cut himself.

Irish Mist

The boys drove in from the city midafternoon. Papa looked happy to see them and got his ideas together about how the three of them could get extra stuff done while they were home. Colb and Andy seemed a bit surprised by the quick spring thaw. Things in Regina were still frozen. It was pretty strange, they thought. I was thinking that too.

I came up with the idea of showing off a bit, maybe make Papa forget about the cat thing. I should do my best to put a special dinner on the table to celebrate us all being together. I wished I had some fresh meat to cook up. I wanted to surprise them all with how much I had learned about keeping house. I went out to the shed where we kept the wringer washer and a chest freezer. It wouldn't be fresh meat, but I knew how to make it taste good. The old contraption was huge and rattled louder than a snake about to strike, but it did its job. I rummaged around in its depths, moving glass containers and brown butcher paper wrapped bundles. I was quite occupied with my meal plans and looking for the perfect ingredients when I heard a bang. Like a gunshot type of bang. I let the lid slam shut and turned to leave the shed. Through the dirty window, I saw Colb run past. He was in a hurry, yelling for Andy to come quick. I went out into the yard. New daffodils were showing on the fresh shoots and the crab trees were starting to bud. *Where had everyone disappeared to now?*

I called the dogs, I called out my brothers' names, I called for Papa. Even the birds were silent. I rushed to the house. The grass had grown long, and my feet

Chapter 1 - The Well

disappeared beneath me. Mama was right where I had left her, talking to herself about recipes and tea towels and flower seeds. She saw me and asked, "Where did your father get to?"

I ran out of the house without answering. Standing on the wide front porch, I searched. Left and right and over by the barn and the other way towards the well. Finally, I saw the group of them, standing with heads bent, beside the well. The barrel of the gun was pointed downwards. The ground felt hard and dry, summer dry, as my feet pounded their way towards them. I did a quick head count. Three men, two dogs. I felt my lungs refill with air. A dead ewe lay at their feet. My eyes followed the trail of blood. There was another body. The feral dog did not move. He had killed his last sheep. Papa went to get his shovel. The dog would need to be buried. Colb and Andy carried the ewe to the barn. The fresh meat would feed us for quite a while.

When I got out of bed on Sunday morning, the dawn had not yet said hello to the day. There was something I had to do. The air was already warm and I dressed quickly. I tiptoed past the boys, who were sleeping on the floor in the main room, their blankets tossed aside. I quietly opened the door and stepped outside. The dogs didn't even lift their heads as I went past. The stars were giving their last light and the moon had already faded. In the dim light, I picked my way around rocks and old fence posts to the well.

Irish Mist

I opened its cover. The hinges creaked at me in protest or warning; I did not care. Despite my fiery spirit, the Irish colleen in me was afraid. I had no understanding of this ghost that had lived in the well, but I had no wish for it to be living in my belly. This was a God-fearing community. Did it not know that? Surely it was obvious by the fancy church on the corner of Main Street. Just as obvious should it be that if it were discovered that I, Colleen, could make wishes come true with such awful consequences, no one would talk to me again. There certainly would not be anyone asking to see my knickers. This had to stop. I had no interest in this kind of crazy-making. I wished *it*, whatever it was, to go back from whence it came. As I stood there, talking in the darkness, the wind picked up. A cold, north wind.

#5 It Never Happened

Colleen frowned into the depths of the well. She tried to make sense of the last few days. Her logical mind decided for her. *It had never happened. It must have been a dream.* She realized that she was standing there, just staring, when a shiver ran through her. She pulled her crocheted shawl tighter across her chest and slammed the cover shut. With a quick turn, she started back to the house. There was no sign of any skirmish involving the feral dog. *Had it ever been there?* It was too dark to see clearly; the dawn was merely a hope in the eastern sky.

The dogs thumped their tails on the rough wood of the porch floor, a signal of the day to come, as she

Chapter 1 - The Well

walked past. She opened the house door and was happy for its welcoming warmth. The boys were sleeping soundly, just as she had left them when she had gone to the well. That part was real enough. They were home and that made her happy. She loved her brothers deeply and had missed them—even their friendly teasing, not that she would ever admit that to them. She hesitated to disturb them with morning sounds, but that thought didn't last but a moment. She started moving about in the kitchen, banging pots and using the hand pump for the water for tea and breakfast things. It sure was going slow! She put fresh wood on the dying embers of the cook stove.

Colb rolled onto his back and pulled the blanket over himself. It had gotten chilly again. He opened one eye and gazed at his sister as she went about her tasks. He had missed her. They were close in age. He watched her movements, noticing for the first time how much she was like their mother. She talked to herself as she fiddled with pots and containers of coffee and flour. When had she grown up? He raised his body on one elbow and offered up a cheery grin. "There's a good lass! I would love a cuppa when you are done there."

Colleen smiled back at him, "It would go much faster if you got your lazy backside over here to help me with the stove. The wood bin is almost empty." Despite the craziness of the last two days, she still held onto her plan for Sunday's dinner. With Mama still in bed, no one would be going to church. It turned into a really good excuse for 'missing'.

Irish Mist

Missing Sunday church service was frowned upon in a small community such as they belonged to. A few years ago, its devout congregation had put forward an expansion plan. The bell tower needed repair, and an addition to the main building could be added at the same time. The schoolroom was getting crowded; it could be moved to ground level. Social hour after the morning service would take place there. The elderly of the congregation were having trouble with the stairs to the basement. All sorts of good reasons for wringing some extra money from the pockets of its followers. They did get their money, and the bell tower had been fixed. It was pretty fancy, as was the new entrance into the building, but the schoolroom had never been moved, and the children continued with their studies in the damp and dim of the stone foundation walls. The AA people still met in the basement on Tuesday evenings: it was like their sins needed to be kept in the dark. A portion of the new section had been turned into office space for the minister. Long tables were stored against the adjacent walls and used for gatherings after services. Colleen focused her attention back to breakfast. Her mind sure could wander. The water would be boiling soon, but she had time to change her clothes to something more practical for housework and to check on Mama.

Mama was asleep. The bandage covering the gash on her head was still clean. The sun was up now, and Colleen pulled back the blue and white gingham curtains. Dust motes sparkled and danced in the fresh light. Papa had already left for the barn: he always said that the cows came first. She picked up discarded

Chapter 1 - The Well

clothes and put them in the hamper. Mama still had not stirred. Perhaps she should make a bit of noise. Then she could ask if Mama was feeling better and put some of her lingering guilt aside. *I must have let the cat in. No one else could have done it,* she thought. She hummed a tune. She cleared her throat. She gently kicked the side of the hope chest at the bottom of the bed. Mama did not move. Now Colleen was getting scared. She leaned over and put her hand on the blue flannel coverlet. She lowered her face to Mama's mouth, and, yes, she was breathing. *Maybe I should let her sleep. I will bring her some tea later.*

#6 Officer Bill

Sunday dinner finally made its way to the table. Colleen had run herself ragged all morning, just trying to do half of what her mother seemed to accomplish with ease. She had no idea that making a meal for five could be so difficult. Andy, who was the oldest, had an appetite like no other and he was getting snarly. All morning he had been underfoot. All he wanted was to have his dinner and get back to the city. He ranted on about it every chance he got, talking on and on instead of bringing in wood or doing something useful. Colb, the practical one, was being his usual cheery and helpful self and had kept busy with farm stuff, figuring out what needed doing. Andy had required telling. Even that didn't work worth a darn. She wished he would smarten up.

Irish Mist

The boiled carrots and roasted potatoes looked pretty good next to the roasted lamb. She had found Mama's stash of dried herbs and had used the rosemary on the meat and potatoes. It smelled even better than it looked. She had forgotten to turn the spuds in the pan and they were burnt on the bottom, but she figured the men were too hungry to notice. They gave thanks for their meal and dug in.

Colleen was worried about Mama. She was still sleeping. She knew that this situation was real, not anything that she had made up in her head. As she thought about things, playing with her fork and moving her vegetables around on her plate, there was a knock on the door. She got up, wiping her hands on her home-sewn apron. The knock came from the side door, where the dogs waited impatiently for the food scraps to be tossed into their bowls. They would have been barking their fool heads off if it weren't for that. Colleen opened the door to see an RCMP officer, looking very official in his perfectly clean and expertly pressed uniform. "Hi Bill! Come on in. We're just finishing up but you are welcome to sit with us. What brings you out from town?" Bill, or Officer Williams as he preferred to be called when he was in uniform, was a friend and school chum of Andy's. He had graduated the year before Andy and had gone on to study law enforcement. It came as a bit of a surprise that he had chosen the law as a career. By Colleen's recollection, Bill had always been the first kid to suggest some kind of fool adventure, usually landing him and all his followers in deep trouble. He claimed it gave him an edge over those criminal

Chapter 1 - The Well

types: he could understand their thinking. Colleen got stuck trying to understand why his father had called him Bill. *Wasn't his last name Williams?* she wondered.

Officer Williams kicked some imaginary dirt off his spit-polished boots and fiddled with the brim of the hat in his gloved hands. "This isn't a social visit, Colleen. I need to speak with your father. Is he here?" Papa, still forking food into his mouth, heard his name called from the porch and came to the door, using his sleeve to wipe the gravy from his mouth. He knew that nothing good came from an RCMP officer at your door on a Sunday, at dinnertime.

It turned out that the feral dog had not been what he had seemed. The neighbour, the next one along the road, had heard the gunshot yesterday and now his dog was missing. Bill, Officer Williams, wanted to know if we had anything to do with that.

Here it was again, staring her in the face. Things that could not be dismissed. First the wind stopped. Then the hens got out. Next was the almost flooded yard. Mama was in bed with a concussion, the boys were home, and the neighbour's dog was dead. And now, there was roasted fresh lamb on the table. Colleen tried to keep her mind from spinning out of control.

What have I done? She put her arms into the sleeves of her coat and went outside.

Irish Mist

#7 Fetching Water

The copper line that ran from the well to the house had started to freeze up again, and Colleen needed water for dishwashing. She retrieved the galvanized pail from its place by the sink. Fetching water was a good excuse to have some thinking time, and she had a lot to think about. It was also a good excuse to leave Officer Williams and Papa to their discussion on the subject of dead sheep and killing dogs. Andy would be seizing this opportunity to eat up any remaining food in the serving bowls. Colb would try to keep the peace. It was always like that. She went out the door, the dogs following at her heels.

Bailey and Jack had been born in the same litter of pups; one was yellow and the other black. Dogs of different colours got along just fine. Folks should take a lesson from them. She couldn't understand why some people thought they were better than others. We all came into the world the same way was her thinking. As she walked across the yard to the well, her mind turned the corner from thinking about dogs and around to thinking about the church-goers that she had met. They seemed to think that they knew better too, like they had some special inside connection to things unseen. Every No-Tell Motel had a bible in the bedside drawer. Someone by the name of Gideon had put them there, so that anyone could read about that stuff. There were bibles at the library, in the church, more bibles than people, by the looks of it. She didn't need to read about it, she already knew about things like that. Always had.

Chapter 1 - The Well

Colleen debated her options as she stood with the rope and brick in her hand. She, quite frankly, was a bit curious as to what might happen when she lifted the hinged cover back. The other half of her mind, the part that Papa controlled, told her to stop, she would only cause more trouble, and hadn't her 'head in the mist' attitude caused enough to go wrong already? Papa had a way of talking, without his having to say a word out loud. Bailey, the yellow Lab, stopped his sniffing around and came up to her. He pushed his wet nose into her hand. Bailey also had a way of talking without using words. She raised the lid.

Colleen dropped the brick, attached to its fraying rope, into the well. The ice layer was not thick and it crashed right through on the first try. She held her breath. Nothing happened. The only thing going on was that, as she kept on waiting, she was running out of breath. Her sense of silly was getting to her, but she was not giving in to such nonsense. If there really was something down there, she should know about it, respect it, and not be little-girl afraid. She called on the fiery spirit that lived within her to give her courage and dropped the pail into the water. Like any other day, it sank and filled with water. No swirling mist, no strange sounds or voices, just water. She pulled on the rope, the bucket rose, and she closed the lid. As she walked back to the house, her feeling of disappointment came as no surprise to her. She always did enjoy a good adventure and now, it was obviously over.

Irish Mist

Bill's patrol car was still in the drive. He must have decided to have a visit after all. She could hear cheery voices coming from the kitchen. It appeared that the men had talked things through and come to an agreement. Andy and Bill were reconnecting after not seeing each other for many years. Bill was encouraging Andy to get out in the world and do something useful, suggesting that what he had been doing in the city was not going to get him anywhere in life. As she took off her brother-boots and coat, Colleen heard Andy say, "I think you've got something there, Bill. I'm leaving early in the morning to go back. I'll do as you suggest and pay a visit to the recruiting centre when I get off work." She could hardly believe her ears. Andy was going to smarten up. *I guess it isn't over after all.*

#8 Monday

Andy and Colb left early in the morning. They had to get back to their life in the city. Andy worked in a grocery store, and Colb was studying mechanics at the college. I was excited for Andy and his plan to become an RCMP officer. Officer Andy was very important sounding. I thought about how, just yesterday, I had wished that he would smarten up.

Mama was still in bed. She wasn't eating anything at all, despite the offerings I had brought to her. I told Papa that he needed to get Dr. McCall to come back out and have another look at her. She was getting worse. If she didn't wake up soon, she was going to starve. He made the phone call before he left for the barn.

Chapter 1 - The Well

I was supposed to be in school. The yellow bus had waited at the end of the drive for several minutes. Mrs. Jansen, the bus driver, had even honked her horn a few times before she drove off. Papa was busy with cows and things. He probably didn't even know that I was still home. Who did he think was going to do all the stuff that Mama did? I guess he would notice if his dinner wasn't on the table.

I needed to make another trip to the well. The pump was still sluggish with ice chips clogging the line. I put on my coat and brother-boots and grabbed the pail. As I stepped off the porch, the dogs circled me. They hoped I had some breakfast bits to share with them, but breakfast hadn't happened yet. I would get to that soon enough. The sky was pure blue, not a cloud in sight. It was a beautiful spring day and the weather seemed to be softening on its own now.

As I walked, the empty pail banging against the side of my leg, I thought about all the other times that I had felt, rather than seen, *things*. There was the day that the Wilson's boy hadn't come home from play. All the near-neighbours had formed a group and gone looking for him. They had come back discouraged and concerned for his well-being. Mr. Wilson was thinking he needed to call the RCMP. When Papa came back from searching around for young Sam and told me that he had not yet been found, I said that I thought he was probably looking for frogs by the far creek.

Irish Mist

Papa hurried back out the door. When he brought Sammy home to his parents, the RCMP had just arrived. They were talking with Mr. and Mrs. Wilson, trying to calm them down. Turned out that Little Sam had been afraid to go home. He had gotten his good clothes muddy and was waiting for them to dry out, so he could scrape the dirt off before his mom saw the mess. I somehow knew where he would be found. Then there was the time that the cows had gotten through a break in the fence and wandered off. I found them too! I also remembered the day when Mrs. MacElhinney had fallen on her way to her car and had lain in the rain for hours. I *felt* her plea for help. I got Colb to drive me over there when she didn't answer her phone, and it was Colb who had called for the ambulance. She spent two weeks in hospital before she could go home. No one had bothered to ask how I had known she was in trouble.

The well looked no different today. Same coiled rope with its brick attached. Same hinged wooden lid. I held my breath. Maybe I shouldn't hold my breath. Maybe I needed to just open the lid. Mama needed to get better. I needed to get back to school. Papa needed his wife. *Please let this work.* I wasn't afraid of the mist, I was afraid that nothing would happen. Maybe it had already happened, and I didn't know about it. Maybe, I should just open the lid. *Oh, for goodness sake, Colleen! Stop your thinking and open the lid!* I opened the lid. Same creaking hinge. I peeked in. A face stared back at me. My face.

Chapter 1 - The Well

#9 The Face in the Well

I looked with disbelief at my reflection in the water. Wait. No. Not a reflection. The face that looked up at me was older, a grown woman. She wore a hint of wrinkles on a face of wisdom, softness, and love. I struggled to connect the vision with my childhood. *I know this woman, this is not me. This is my Aunt Irene. What had happened to her? Why am I seeing her face in the water?*

Time seemed to hover without substance as I tried to find the memory. It came to me from a great distance, so very long ago. I was barely tall enough to see over the top of the harvest table that is still in use in the house today. I could not have been more than four. The scene's edges sharpened as I saw myself as a child with auburn-hued braids and bright blue eyes, a patched pair of denim overalls that I had yet to properly grow into, and someone else. Yes! An older woman, sitting beside Mama, reaching out with warm hugs and soft encouragement. *This was Aunt Irene. Where had she gone?* I could not find the answer within my mind. I would have to ask Papa.

I continued to stare at the face, mesmerized by the mist that formed it. I moved my voice to my mind and asked my aunt why she was reaching out from the water, from this strange place. The answer was simple, "Because I need you."

Loud shouts disturbed my thoughts. I heard my name called out, demanding my return to the now of things. It was Papa, yelling for me to come quickly. I closed the lid, forgetting my pail and my conversation, and ran in the direction of Papa's voice. Something was very wrong. The dogs were barking furiously. There was an ambulance in the drive, and Dr. McCall was there too. He was directing two men dressed in hospital clothes into the house. They were going to take Mama away!

My brain twisted and turned as I tried to absorb the reality in front of me and understand the fantasy of my mind. It was quite the task. Auntie's voice broke through my thoughts, beckoning me back to the well. Somehow, the sense that she could tell me what to do came clearly. I needed to have the right wish. The wrong one could have awful consequences. I was barely 14. How did I know that I could do anything? Boil water and sweep the porch, yes, maybe catch a fish if I got lucky. I would still have to ask for help to bait the hook—*isn't that what brothers are for?* Somehow I was going to have to find a way to fix this. Mama just couldn't die.

The ambulance pulled away with the doctor following in his car. Papa had climbed into the back of the ambulance and shouted at me just as the doors were closing. I did not hear what he said, but the fear in his voice did not need words. I stood there, the road dust swirling, the dogs barking, the vehicles disappearing on their way to town. *Colleen, you had better do this right,* I told myself as I went back to the well and opened the lid again. "Auntie," I called. "It's me, Colleen. Why do you need me? What do you want me to do? Mama is sick. She hit her head and it's all my fault because I was selfish and didn't want to do chores! You have got

Chapter 1 - The Well

to help me!" It had all rushed out in one long breath. Then, like a light going on in the dark, I realized that my aunt had asked for *my* help. Perhaps I ought to be listening and not talking. Perhaps it would all weave together. I willed myself to be still.

Auntie's voice spoke to my mind. "I need to be free of this dark, damp place. I need to be free to live again, to rise from these cold vapors and feel the warmth of the sky. I need you to be my way. Only then can I truly help you. We can live together, one body, two minds. No one will know of your sacrifice but us. Please Colleen, you are my hope." I felt my spirit acquiesce. The mist rose towards me, circling me, and found its mark. It warmed its place in my belly and settled in where it had been before. As the two of us became one, I realized what I had been missing. This was to be my life: I had been able to see things unseen, and now I could call on them to use as I needed—my very own Irish Mist. My mind finally understood what my heart had known forever. There was no turning back now. I wished Mama would hurry up and get well. Tomorrow was laundry day.

#10 The Flannel Nightgown

Colleen coiled the length of rope with its attached broken piece of brick and laid it beside the well. She shouldn't need that for much longer. The ice would soon be gone: they were into April now. Soon she would be seeing fields of bright yellow as mustard plants came into bloom. She picked up her pail of water and smiled to herself as she made her way back to the house. As she filled the kettle and put it on the stove to boil, she wondered how long it would be before she heard any news from the hospital. She fed the dogs and gave them fresh water. While the tea steeped, she collected the morning eggs from the henhouse. The cows were out grazing and would not need attention until suppertime. *Surely, Papa would be back by then.*

The rest of the day passed quickly. There was always lots to be done on a farm, even one as small as theirs. They didn't keep a lot of livestock, just some milkers and a dozen hens to keep them in eggs. There was a pair of goats and a very old donkey that seemed to have always been there. Thanks to the neighbour's dog, there were a few less sheep to worry about. He had been helping himself to the herd for quite a while. Apparently, he had a taste for lamb chops. Most of the money that came in to support them was from Papa's disability cheques. There was enough to live on, and Colleen didn't pay much attention to the rest of the details. Her parents looked after those things.

It was getting dark by the time Papa got a ride home. It was a long way from the hospital, and he was thankful that Dr. McCall lived nearby and was coming this way anyway. He was bone tired from travel and concern. He didn't ask about the cows or anything else. He was too worried about Mama to notice much. Hospitals were to be avoided; people died in them. Mama had been given fluids by IV and when he had left for home, she had been awake. The doctor wanted to keep her overnight for observation and most likely she would be back home tomorrow. Colleen nodded her head and smiled. She already knew everything would be all right.

Chapter 1 - The Well

She put together some supper for the two of them and cleaned up the kitchen. The neighbour's boys had taken care of the milking and corralled the rest of the livestock securely in the barn. The dogs were already curled up nose to tail, and the moon was rising in the dark sky when she went to her room and got ready for the night.

Her double bed fit perfectly beneath the sloping wall of the high-pitched roof. The walls were painted strawberry pink and the window frame in the dormer was pure white. Mama had made the quilt for her, its squares of different spring flowers all sewn together with a beautiful maroon border. She had worked really hard on it during many an evening. Her black and gold Singer sewing machine hummed along as radio sounds filled the background. Colleen loved those sounds, all of them. It was what home sounded like.

She could see the clouds multiplying as they drifted in from the west. She pulled her favourite flannel nightie out of the cedar-lined drawer. It had been a gift a few years back, so long ago that she couldn't remember whom it was from. It had little pink roses with green leaves printed on its soft surface. There was a small satin flower on each side of the collar and pearl buttons that went a quarter of the way down the front. Even though she had grown taller, it still fell below her knees. It was as comforting as warm milk, kind of like her Aunt Irene. *Maybe it had been her aunt who had given it to her?* She would have to remember to ask. Colleen settled into bed with the library book she had been reading before all this craziness had started, days ago.

Irish Mist

The rain started after midnight. She was awakened by its tinny concerto playing on the steel roof over her head. She had always liked the rain. She loved its cleansing sound, fresh water rinsing off the debris of the world in a way that soap and scrubbing could not do. She loved its smell, how the droplets stirred up the sleeping earth and let loose its mustiness. It was raining hard. Papa had said that it might keep up for days. She had heard the stories of the floods in this part of the province. People had died after being swept away by the turbulent waters of a flash flood. It was just awful how that had happened. She started to worry that it might happen again. If she kept on worrying, she would never get back to sleep. She tried to focus on something positive. No laundry to be done in the rain. There would be other things for her to be busy with, things she enjoyed more than washing stinky clothes. She still needed to talk with Papa about Aunt Irene. Colleen fluffed her pillow and went back to sleep, the lullaby of the distant thunder and falling rain calming her fears.

#11 Andrew Malachi Timmons

Andrew Malachi Timmons had been born 19 years ago on a cold and snowy afternoon in the month of March in Back of Beyond, Saskatchewan. He had been born at home, in the old farmhouse where his mother's parents, Claire and Walter McNab had lived, right up until they moved into town. When they retired, they had passed the farm on to their daughter Edith and her husband. The regional hospital was a ways away and Dr. McCall had figured that the firstborn of the Timmons' three children was in a hurry to come into the world.

Chapter 1 - The Well

He thought it would be best if Mama delivered her baby at home—no point in complicating matters by giving birth in the back seat of his car.

The family homestead had been built in the early 1900s. There were thousands of lakes in Saskatchewan, and the McNabs had picked a spot backing on a creek that fed the lakes close by. Grandpa McNab had taught Andy to fish when he was young. He knew there were lots of good fishing places around. Lots of birds too. When the geese returned from their winter homes in the south, the sky would be full of their honking and carrying on. Mama told the kids to always wear a hat in the spring.

There was something special about the lakes and the surrounding wetlands. Birds of all kinds migrated there. The Salt Flats of Saskatchewan were famous for their geese. It was a dangerous place to play during the spring thaw. There were so many creeks and streams that fed the lakes, and the area was prone to flash floods.

Andy drove his small Honda back to the city on Monday morning. He dropped off his brother at the apartment that they shared and then went directly to the grocery store where he worked stocking shelves and collecting shopping carts. Colb would find his own way to classes that afternoon, by bus. He was taking courses to become a mechanic. Colb's plan was to return home when he was done with his studies and find work at the co-op repairing farm machinery. He could live at home, give Papa a hand with the crops, and save his money to buy his own car. Maybe someday he would have his own place. Perhaps the sweet young thing that worked as assistant to Mrs. Kovetski at the post office would like him if he had a car.

Andy didn't think Colb had any idea what kind of special crops Papa was growing. He was going to let his brother find that out for himself. In the meantime, Colb could work on his own dreams. Andy was going to be a law enforcement officer. Hopefully, no one else knew what his parents did to supplement their income.

When Andy finished work for the day, he drove over to the recruiting centre. His friend Bill had given him a few good ideas about making a future for himself. Andy had felt he had been without direction for a while now. After what had happened 10 years ago, he just couldn't seem to get his act together. He had wandered around lost in his own thoughts for the most part. He spent his time eating and sleeping and stocking the store shelves; he played video games or fiddled with his collection of old stamps. Not much else interested him. Not even pretty ladies. It wasn't as if he had "other interests"— he just wasn't interested in anyone.

Colb said he was weird. Andy didn't think he was all that weird. Stuck was more like it. He still blamed himself for the accident. Something had lit a spark in him when Bill Williams had come in to talk to Papa about the neighbour's dog. He looked good in his uniform and his pride in his appearance showed. He looked... confident. Like he had found his place in the world, energized by the knowledge that he, Bill Williams, could make a difference in the lives of his fellow man. For the first

Chapter 1 - The Well

time in a long time, Andy wanted something other than survival for himself. He thought that maybe the time had come for him to do that, to move forward with his life and give up the ghosts of his past. He could do this. Andrew Malachi Timmons took a deep breath, opened the door to the recruitment centre and readied himself for his future. The young woman at the reception desk asked if she could be of help. She sure was pretty. The new-looking nameplate sitting in front of her on the tidy desk said, *Miss M.R.F. Byrne-Calder.*

#12 Irene

Colleen lay in bed. The white eyelet curtains of the dormer window moved ever so slightly with the breeze that came from a steady downpour of cold rain. She rolled herself over so she could see between the cotton panels to the outside. The steel grey sky stared back at her, telling her quite clearly not to expect anything different for the rest of the day. Her fuzzy slippers and terry cloth housecoat would not keep her warm until she got the stove going in the kitchen, and she reluctantly pulled on her jeans and a thick knit sweater. She knew she had slept in. The morning light and the rooster had never failed her before, but her bedside clock told her that "never" happened sometimes. As she went down the stairs, Irene said good morning.

Colleen was so startled by the greeting that she almost lost her footing. She sat down on the bottom step. *Had she heard right?* Her aunt's voice came to her again, more clearly this time, now that her attention had been redirected from breakfast thoughts.

Irish Mist

"I said good morning," Irene repeated. "Did you forget that I am here?"

"Um, maybe," answered Colleen in a small voice. "Aunt Irene? Is that really you?" Colleen felt her head nod. *What??* She was sure she had not done that. Suddenly, she felt very dizzy.

Irene chided her, "Damn it, girl! You have forgotten to breathe!" Aunt Irene always had been a no-nonsense type of person: nothing there had changed. The fact that Colleen had not seen her since she was a little girl until yesterday, yes, that had been a change. The fact that her aunt was now talking to her was even more of a change. There needed to be a serious conversation between the two occupants of this body, and Irene nodded her agreement. But first, Colleen needed to get the fire going and breakfast cooking. Papa would be looking for his oatmeal when he came in from milking the cows. Today, hopefully, Mama would be coming home from the hospital. She needed to prepare for that and have a meal ready. It was a long drive into the city. They would not be back before early afternoon at best. With the weather being so bad, it might take even longer. The rain would be swelling the rivers and there might be detours in place. Such an awful day to have to be out and about.

Arthur came in from the barn and hardly said a word as he shovelled down his hot cereal. He filled his mug from the teapot and looked at his daughter, almost sizing her up, as he stirred in milk and sugar. "I'm going to be awhile," he said, still stirring his tea. "I have some errands to run before I get to the hospital. Hopefully I

Chapter 1 - The Well

will be bringing Ma home tonight. I don't see why not; she's doing fine. Only observation, the doctor told me. Can you see to a meal for us all and get the Henckel boys to look after the milking again? We are so lucky to have such good neighbours, don't you think?" He paused, waiting for his next thought to exit his mouth. "Colleen! Are you listening? You look like you've seen a ghost. I'm talking to you. You need to pay attention. Get your head out of the mist!"

"Yes, Papa. I heard you. I will do what you ask. Please bring Mama home. I can't bear for her not to be here."

Arthur nodded, put his rain jacket over his thick Irish wool sweater, his favourite tweed cap on his head, and went out the door. Colleen could hear the Ford truck start up and spit gravel as it moved towards the #6 Highway.

Colleen poured herself another cup of tea. She sat at the oak table, the now empty bowls with their congealing oatmeal bits still waiting to be put in the sink. She leaned back in her chair and pushed a strand of wayward hair off her forehead. She was alone now, except for the dogs. Except for Aunt Irene. Would now be a good time to have that conversation? Immediately as the thought formed, Irene responded with a comment of her own, "Yes, that would be lovely, but could I have a bit more sugar in my tea, please?"

Irish Mist

#13 Girl Talk

The dirty dishes could wait. Colleen thought that talking with Aunt Irene was far more important than housework. She had so many questions; she was devising a mental list. The crazy part of that was that Irene was answering her as fast as she could think them up! It was all becoming a jumble in her mind, and she needed to slow things down. She got up from her seat at the table and refilled the kettle. She looked back, thinking she really should put the bowls in the sink to soak, and Irene was now sitting in the spot that Colleen had just vacated, looking pleased as punch to at last have her human form returned to her.

Irene looked the same as she had when Colleen was four. The same kindly face with young wrinkles barely starting to show at the corners of her blue-grey eyes. The same warm smile and straight white teeth. Her auburn hair had a lovely wave to it and fell down her back in a glossy mane. She was as beautiful as always. "Now, how does a woman live in the depths of a well for ten years and still look lovely?" That was the first question Colleen asked out loud, more to herself than to Irene. They (they were a "they" now it seemed) were alone in the house. It was pouring down rain. No one was about to come knocking on the door. Colleen gave in to her curiosity and let her inhibitions leave her, just like the thought of doing dishes.

Irene said in a patient voice, "You best be filling the teapot— 'tis quite the tale." Irene had indeed waited a long ten years for a cup of tea and the opportunity to

Chapter 1 - The Well

sit in a warm kitchen with good company. "Well," she started, in her faint Irish brogue, "I suppose I should tell you about the accident; you'd be wanting to know. I don't think your father is about to talk about it, even if you could pin him down long enough to have a conversation. He's a busy one, for sure, always doing something. Andrew knows all about that.

"Speaking of your brother, I think the poor boy still believes that he was somehow at fault. No one else was there that day, no one to bear witness and help him understand. He was just a lad, trying to do something nice for his Mama. It was such a rainy day, same time of year too. It was the day before Edith's birthday. It's coming up soon, isn't it? Andrew was nine, his young mind busy with frogs and birds and things, and he had forgotten all about his ma's birthday. Arthur had dropped a hint at supper the night before when Edith had been busy at the sink. The next morning I had stopped by to get some fresh eggs and milk. Andrew offered to help me get the eggs, and while we were in the coop, he asked me to drive him to town. He gave me his little boy smile that always did melt my heart and I said yes." Irene stirred an extra shake of sugar from the jar into her tea. She paused.

Colleen could tell by the frown on her aunt's face that this was difficult for her. As she sat beside Irene, the rain drumming on the roof and the wood stove going cold, she felt that so many pieces of the puzzle, which had never seemed like a puzzle before, were now being laid out in front of her. Things were starting to make sense. She had been far too young at the time to see the shift in her universe as Andy spent more and more time alone in the room that he shared with Colb. He had stopped joining in the games of tag and makeshift baseball in the front yard. If he wasn't in his room, then he was out in the fields with Papa.

Nanny and Grandad had moved into town. Colleen remembered missing them. Nanny had often made special ginger cookies for the kids, with double ginger. The kitchen had smelled like heaven, or what Colleen's idea of heaven was. Those people at the church talked about streets paved with gold. She wanted her streets to be lined with gingerbread men! She focused her attention back on her aunt. "Did you go to the store? Did Andy get his gift? Why did you go away after that? What happened, Auntie?" she asked.

"Well, as I said, it was an awful, rainy day. It was early spring, so the creeks and streams were overfull with rushing water. It really was a bad idea to go out in such conditions, but Andrew looked so cute, with his hair falling over his eyes and that winsome little boy face. The wee lad looked like it would break his heart if he didn't have a gift for his mama on her birthday. So I thought up some excuse for taking him out with me. I had him safely buckled in the back seat, just like he was supposed to be.

We started off to town. The roads were bad, and I could hardly see out the windshield, even with the wipers going so fast. That's when he tells me that he gets carsick if the window isn't down. I told him he was going to get wet, but he said that water was a

Chapter 1 - The Well

better choice than breakfast all over him. Well, he was right for sure, so I gave him permission to put down his window as far as it would go. That is probably what saved his life. About a mile later, he says he is going to lose his breakfast anyway and did I have a bag or something. I only took my eyes off the road for a second, but I guess I must have swerved a bit when I reached back to give him the emergency potty that I always kept under my seat."

Irene was crying now. Colleen reached for the shawl, hanging from the back of the chair, to warm her shoulders. As she wrapped it around her aunt, she gave her a hug. She felt so real. She thought ghosts would be wispy, like your hands would go right through them, but that didn't happen. Seemed that she didn't know a lot about ghosts, but she was sure that Aunt Irene had gone over that horrible day in her mind a zillion times, as she was locked into her own hell. Colleen waited for her to continue, but she stopped there, and Colleen did not have the heart to ask for more. Irene's slim shoulders heaved with the sobs of a decade as her niece sat beside her, her tea gone cold.

#14 Arthur Cadwyn Timmons

Arthur finished up at the hardware store and headed for the pharmacy. He had a lot of things on his mind and was trying to figure out where he was going to put all his supplies when he went into the hospital to get his wife. He still had a few places to go because he couldn't get everything he needed in one store. He had to spread his shopping around. That way, no one would get suspicious. The lockbox in the bed of the truck would work for an hour or so, and really, he wasn't buying anything strange. It was the quantities that might raise an eyebrow of someone in the know.

As Arthur went from store to store, he thought about Edith. He hoped that she would be sitting in the truck beside him shortly, so they could get home and get back to the business of farming and the rest of the things that kept them in cash. Edith ran the business end of things, and she made sure that the books looked right if anyone cared to have a look. He was almost positive that the kids knew nothing about the real source of their income. Kids just cared that there was food on the table and gas in the car to get them where they wanted to go. He figured that they were too busy with their own teenage lives to notice that the sale of goat cheese and sheep's wool was hardly enough to keep them in cash, and there was always lots of cash around.

Andy knew the ins and outs of things, but he was the only one, outside of Irene, God rest her soul, and Edith. Their eldest son was an adult now, even though he still looked like a kid, and it was okay that he was involved with adult stuff. Arthur and Edith needed a runner to the city and Andy was the perfect choice. They had bought him the old-but-reliable Honda and paid him well for his trouble of going back and forth more often. He had lots of contacts at the store where he worked and so far, no one suspected the box boy of doing anything other than packing and unpacking boxes.

Chapter 1 - The Well

Arthur thought back to the events of ten years ago. Andy had been so needy after Irene had died. It had been an awful time. He hadn't been able to move on from that horrible day. The poor kid had managed to swim his way out of the sinking car before it had been pulled downstream in the torrent of water. Irene had not been so lucky, and the whole family had felt the loss of Edith's younger sister. Their world changed that day, and the fingers of blame and grief had poked big holes into their once happy lives. Irene had only been in her early thirties, so full of the energy of life. She should have been married by then, but she had been too busy with other things to be looking at men. There were plenty of them that looked at her; she was such a ray of sunshine, her smile lit up a room and her voice always held cheer. She had worked as a clerk in the municipal office, but what she had really wanted was to go back to school to become a chemist. It was she who had come up with the idea of the family business. It had seemed a bit of a surprise that she had thought of it, but she had been right. This was a way to pay for her university education, and it would benefit the whole family. It was the perfect location and the perfect opportunity. No one would be looking.

Arthur pulled into the parking lot of the hospital and picked a spot for himself as far away from the entrance as could be. He stored his purchases in the secure metal toolbox in the truck bed and went inside. Hospitals gave him the willies. He pushed the button on the elevator for the fourth floor. The nurses' station was a busy place, and it took a few minutes to find out if Edith would be released. The charge nurse delivered

Irish Mist

the good news that the patient would be going home today, adding a hefty dose of caution to her statement. For the next few days, Edith would require some extra care that could easily happen outside of hospital. She handed him a sheath of instructions that he promised to read later. He walked down the hall to his wife's room, tucking the myriad of papers under his arm, a smile of relief on his face and a lightness to his steps. He rounded the corner to see Edith sitting up in the bed. She looked very pale; he knew that the hospital gown was not meant to be flattering, but frankly, she looked awful to him. The bandage on her face had been removed. Steri-Strips, placed like railway ties, outlined the long gash on her forehead. The blue and purple bruise that spread across her forehead didn't help her appearance one little bit. The IV line was gone too, freeing her arm, and she reached out to grasp his calloused hand.

In quick order, he had Edith dressed in the warm clothes he had brought from home, found her a wheelchair, and was pushing the elevator button for the ground floor. He couldn't get out of there fast enough.

#15 Truck Talk

By the time Arthur came out of the exit doors of the hospital, the rain had slowed to a drizzle. He wheeled the chair, with Edith slumped in it, around the large puddles, through the rows filled with vehicles, and over to where he had parked his truck at the far perimeter of the lot. He gave a quick glance at the lockbox and saw that it was still secure. Edith needed a lot of help getting

Chapter 1 - The Well

into her seat. Her balance was off, and he had to almost lift her in, he was so afraid she would fall. That would surely complicate matters if hospital staff had to come and take her back inside. He buckled the seat belt for her and looked around for a place to put the wheelchair. He left it in the empty parking space next to him, hoping it wouldn't roll into another car. He wondered why there weren't wheelchair return spots, like there were for cart returns. He thought that would be a great idea. He put the truck in gear and navigated his way back onto the #6 Highway, latching his own seat belt as he drove.

They sat in silence as the rain turned to fog and Arthur had to back off the gas pedal. "It's going to take forever to get home, love. Are you managing all right?"

Edith turned her head slowly and looked at her husband. "That's okay, Art, as long as we get there safe. I am in no mood for any more accidents. You might be smart to slow down a bit more. This is not a race to the finish line."

He ignored the rub. "I've asked Colleen to fix us some supper, and she's supposed to get the Henckel boys to come and look after the cows. I'm going to be busy unloading the truck when we get home. I stopped for supplies before I picked you up. I didn't think you'd want me doing errands while you had to wait in the rain. I got enough stuff to keep us busy for a while." He talked on about farm-related matters while Edith stared into the surrounding gloom of the fog. She had already tuned him out and was occupied with her own jumble of thoughts and emotions.

Irish Mist

The business worried her. She didn't like it that Andy had to be involved. She wondered how long it would be before they would be asking Colb to pitch in. She wanted him to finish his schooling. He would make a great mechanic. Colb was forever taking things apart and fiddling with bits of things to make other things. Creative he was, and such a happy boy, always with a smile on his face. Andy had been like that too, before Irene had died. Colleen was still young, but that girl had some pretty strong opinions about things. She was so like her aunt. They even looked alike. Edith let her mind wander as the miles added up behind them. She had such a terrible headache now; it was too hard to think. She closed her eyes and listened to the slap of the windshield wipers as they played a song in her head, pulling her into sleep.

Arthur had a hand on the wheel and his eyes on the road, but his mind had drifted off somewhere else when he had come to realize that Edith was no longer listening to his verbal list of Have-To, Should, and Maybe. He had been talking to himself for a while now. He thought about all the stress he was under. He had to make money. There were lots of things that needed doing. Perhaps he could get Colb to help. He would have to remember to call him. He should get onto fixing the plumbing and digging a new supply line from the well, five feet down where it wouldn't freeze. They needed to be able to use that damn pump all winter. Maybe this year he would put a furnace under the house. He was tired of the cold that seeped into his bones from the Saskatchewan winter. He wasn't even 50 yet, but some days he felt old. He mused on as the fog deepened and he was forced to slow down even more.

Chapter 1 - The Well

When he finally made the turn into their driveway, he stopped to check the mailbox. As was his habit, he quickly leafed through its contents before he continued up to the house. Amidst the advertisements and bills was a notice from the post office. He had a package waiting for pickup. He would have to drive back into town again tomorrow.

#16 The Far-Back Shed

I heard, rather than saw, the truck come up the drive to the house. I opened the outside door to the porch and watched, feeling helpless and very guilty, as Papa helped Mama inside. She seemed so wobbly on her feet and leaned heavily on Papa's arm, the plaster strips on her forehead a glaring reminder of what had happened. He walked her down the hall to the bedroom where I had the covers turned down on the freshly made bed and a clean chamber pot under its

Irish Mist

frame. In anxious anticipation of her return home, I had scoured the bloodstains from the pine plank floor and aired the room. The farmwork was almost done for the day, and there was a stew simmering on the back of the stove. I was exhausted, and it was only four o'clock! I helped Mama put on the pretty nightgown I had laid out for her and went back to the kitchen to make her some tea.

Papa had already disappeared to the shed, the one at the far back, by the creek. He was probably going to be busy for a while unloading his recent purchases from the truck and putting them all away on the shelves. That was where he kept things like paint, acetone, weed killer and fertilizer, toxic stuff he called it. I didn't go back there. Papa said it was dangerous. I might breathe in something that would make me sick. He always wore one of those funny-looking masks when he was inside that shed. Sometimes, at night, I could see the light on out there, and I could see him through the shed's dirty window, fiddling around and mixing stuff, probably to help the crops grow better or maybe keep the locusts from eating the plants. He ran an extension cord from the barn to the shed so he had electricity. For water, he had three or four hoses connected to each other to make one long hose, but he only turned that on when he was out there. One day I had seen him carrying a small space heater inside. I guess he didn't want the paint to freeze.

We had a few outbuildings on the property, and I didn't worry about going in any of the other places except for the long drop privy behind the barn. That

Chapter 1 - The Well

was just gross! The men used that when they had to relieve themselves during the day. It smelled worse than pig shit in there, and we didn't own any pigs! Mama and I used the one close to the house. We poured lime down the hole so it didn't smell so bad. There was a bathroom inside the house too, but it didn't work in the wintertime when the lines were frozen. Papa had talked about putting a furnace in for years, but it hadn't happened yet. Keeping myself clean was a chore all by itself. Most of the kids at school had hot running water! I'm not sure why we hadn't come to having it ourselves. "Maybe next year," Papa always said.

Arthur busied himself putting things away in the shed. He turned on the portable radio and listened to the news as he made sure that all the items from the truck went into the proper places on the metal shelving. That way he could tell when he was running low on something, and he could get Andy to get more for him. He hoped that the package waiting at the post office was from his nephew in North Dakota. Darryl usually sent him one each month, the most he could do without arousing suspicion. The one from last month had not shown up, and Arthur hoped that it had just gotten lost in the mail, rather than being held up at the Canadian border. He didn't need any trouble with that on top of dealing with Edith's injury. Now where had he put that set of instructions the nurse had given him? Probably not important anyway. He went back to sorting his packages.

Irish Mist

#17 Tea in a Fancy Cup

Mama looked pretty in the peach flannel nightie with its touch of lace around the collar, and the colour of the fabric helped put a bit of brightness in her cheeks. She smiled when I brought in the old wood tray with a hot cup of tea in a fancy china cup with a matching plate. I had made her a small sandwich with fresh goat cheese and sprinkled a bit of cinnamon on it to give it some sweetness. It had been cut fancy too, with the crusts removed. I figured I had some time to sit with her while she ate before I needed to get busy in the kitchen again. I felt bad about what had happened and wanted to say I was sorry for having let the cat in.

As I watched her take a tentative sip of the hot tea, I noticed Irene take up a spot on the other side of the bed. My jaw dropped open in surprise. I looked over at Mama, who was still holding the delicate teacup pressed to her mouth. *Did she not see her sister? I could see her plain as day!* Irene made the hush sign with her finger to her lips. She told my mind to be still. She wanted to sit with her Edith. She had missed her so much. For right now, that was all that needed to happen. Irene was crying again, big wet tears falling in her lap as she sat on the blue coverlet, cherishing the sweet moment of being with her sister after so many years apart. I left them to their time together, wondering if Mama would ever see Irene as I did or if she could even feel her presence. I sure hoped so. I went off to feed the dogs and check on the stew.

Chapter 1 - The Well

Colleen tried to sort through the thousand and one thoughts going through her mind. She pumped water into the sink and filled the kettle again, put more wood in the stove, and stirred the stew. She dumped kibble into the dogs' bowls and set the table. She waved to the Henckel boys going by as they left the barn for home. She gave the bell that hung on the back porch a good clanging to let Papa know that supper was ready. She washed and dried her hands for the third time, and she still was no closer to understanding the mystery of Irene and the well.

Edith sipped her tea and took in the familiarity of her bedroom. The blue and white gingham curtains were still tied back, but the sun hadn't managed to break through the heavy cloud cover of the day and there was nothing to be seen through the fog. The blue flannel coverlet matched the blue of the curtains perfectly. She had been so proud of her purchases from the Sears Catalogue when she realized that they paired so well, hard to do that from just a picture. They were almost new. She loved the crisp look of cotton gingham. That had been one of Andy's first drives into town when he was 16.

He had picked up the parcels for her from the cupboard-sized catalogue office shared with the feed store. Now Colb was starting to drive, and it wouldn't be long before Colleen was behind the wheel as well. Her eyes lingered on the fancy picture frame decorated with fabric hearts that her daughter had given her for Mother's day when she was in grade school. Beside it was the carved horse on slightly off-centred rockers that Colb had made in shop class. Andy's turned wood bowl was sitting on the top of Arthur's highboy dresser. It was home for his tie clip, loose change, fallen-off buttons waiting to be resewn, and a crumpled church bulletin, probably there from the baptism they had attended a few months back.

Despite her relentless headache, she felt better. It was good to be home. Nothing like a cuppa tea and a sandwich to help with that. There was something else, she couldn't put her finger on it, but something different about the room. She searched again but found nothing amiss or more than what was there before. Whatever it was, it was a feel-good thing. She took another bite of her fancy-cut sandwich and admired the lovely china that it had been served on. She would have to tell Colleen that she didn't hold her to blame for her fall. It had happened, and that was that. She didn't want her to go through the same guilt that Andy had suffered after Irene had died. Irene. That was it. That was what was different. She moved her hand to touch the silver bracelet that she always wore on her wrist. It was gone.

#18 Table Talk

Arthur came in the back door and hung up his coat. He moved to the sink, where he washed up with the cake of soap that looked almost as grimy as his hands. "Colleen! Don't we have a decent bar of soap? How am I supposed to get clean if the soap is dirty?"

Chapter 1 - The Well

I looked up from the pot of stew, ladle in one hand and serving bowl in the other. "Well, if you want a new bar of soap, then you will have to get it yourself. Can you not see that I have my two hands full?" I couldn't believe I had just talked to my father that way. If this new attitude of mine kept up, I was going to be calling him Arthur soon, instead of Papa, and that would not be good. Things were getting very strange. I needed to put my earth back on its rightful course, and I had no idea how to do that. Perhaps Aunt Irene could help. It was she who had started this mess.

I put the bowls on the table and fetched a new bar of soap for Papa from under the cabinet. "I'm sorry, Papa. I should not have spoken to you with disrespect. I don't know what is wrong with me this past week. I have been doing all sorts of odd things and—"

Papa interrupted me, "We will give thanks for our food first, Colleen. Then you can go on with your ramblings."

I lowered my head and listened as Papa said the blessing. For a man who went to church only on special occasions, he sure was religious. It was confusing to me. I never knew when he would pull out some verse of scripture and stand on it like it was the rock of God. Next thing I knew, he was doing something that was against everything I had ever learned in Sunday school. Papa had his own way of thinking, that was for sure. The good thing in all this was that he did not believe in long-drawn-out prayers. He was pretty quick when it came around to eating his

Irish Mist

supper while it was still hot. Tonight he seemed to have a bit more to say. As I sat, waiting for Papa to sum up, I looked down at my hands. I was wearing Mama's favourite bracelet. Papa had taken it off her arm when she got to the hospital. He didn't trust anyone at that place and was afraid that it would be stolen. That was another surprise, coming from a man who never locked a door and left the keys in the truck. I guess the city was different. I hadn't been there much except to visit Colb and Andy a few times. I was roused from my thoughts by a loud, "Amen!" I looked up. "This smells good, Colleen. Aren't you going to eat?" Papa picked up his knife and slathered a layer of butter on his bread.

"I'm sorry, Papa. Yes. I was just thinking. It's getting warmer now, and the pump in the kitchen seems to be working fine. Could you, maybe, turn on the water to the bathroom? It would make it so much easier for Mama. I am afraid she will fall going down the porch steps to get to the privy."

Papa considered the request as he spooned stew into his mouth. He took another piece of bread and spread the butter even thicker this time. "I suppose so. Shouldn't be too difficult to get that done tomorrow. I will take a look at what I need after I am done with the milking. I have to make a trip to town anyway. I could pick up plumbing supplies at the co-op." He stopped talking after that and sopped up the gravy in the bottom of the bowl with the last of the bread. He pushed back his chair, put on his coat, and went outside. So much for interesting conversation.

Chapter 1 - The Well

I finished my own supper and started to clear the table. When I looked up from the plates, there was Irene, sitting in Mama's spot. "Hello," she said. I was getting used to seeing her now, and this time I wasn't startled by her appearance. "Your Mama can't see me. You know that, right? I saw the look on her face though, and she knows that I am here. I'm so glad of that. It would be torture if I was not able to, at the least, have her feel me beside her. She's quite ill. Her mind is all jumbled, I can sense that. Must be, because words don't come out of her mouth as they should. Did the doctor not do anything for her? I can't believe that all this is going on. And your father, what is going on with him? He hardly spends any time with her. You'd think he would be worried. He's gone back out to the shed. I wish I could give him a piece of my mind! Lots to say, eh? For someone who just climbed out of a well!" She stopped for breath, noticing the look of bewilderment on my face.

"Auntie, about the well, how did that happen? I mean, how did you get in there in the first place? Why were you in there? What made you decide to come out? I have so many questions. Can we please talk?"

Irene looked at her niece. "Better put the kettle on to boil."

I rose from the table, collected the remaining supper dishes and walked to the sink to do as my aunt had asked. Kettle in hand, I pondered to myself, *Do ghosts eat? Should I have offered her some supper? Am I being rude?* I let out a big sigh. More questions, always more questions. Soon I will have some answers. As that thought left me, the loud dull thump of something hitting the floor came from the back room. I let go of the kettle and rushed down the hall.

#19 The Silver Bracelet

Mama was lying on the floor, her soaking wet nightgown wrapped around her legs. A puddle was spreading out from the overturned chamber pot. Irene had followed me from the kitchen and now stood in the doorway, a look of dismay on her face. "Come help me!" I pleaded with her. "I can't lift her by myself. And she's all wet. Get a clean nightie from the drawer. Doesn't matter which one." To the end of that sentence, I added a hurried *Please!* to the end of the sentence.

Irene didn't move. She just stood there looking at Mama. "I can't," she said. "I'm new at this, remember? You are going to have to do this yourself. I'm here with you. I'll think. You lift. Thinking counts as help." The last of it sounded more like she was trying to convince herself rather than encourage me.

As I did what had to be done, I was getting angry. Angry and frustrated and confused and, yes, angry! It was all too much. Too much trouble. Too much unknown. Too much to do. Just. Too. Much. Before the thinking part of my brain could stop the feeling part of my brain from exploding, my mouth opened and I could hear myself yelling at Aunt Irene. I must have gone on for quite a while. Mama's voice cut through my tirade. "Colleen! Just exactly who are you yelling at?"

Chapter 1 - The Well

I stared at her with one of those deer-in-the-headlights looks on my face. Mama had the fresh nightie half over her head and was struggling, trying to get her arms in the sleeves. It was almost comical, seeing her face peeking out of the neck opening with the plasters on her forehead and her hair sticking out in all directions. But it wasn't funny at all, and I instantly felt ashamed of myself. "I am so sorry, Mama. I shouldn't have been yelling. I'm sure your head hurts and me yelling is just making things worse. Let me help you." I guided her arms where they needed to go, pulled the hem of the nightie down to cover her body and smoothed her hair back in place. I pulled the covers over her legs." I love you, Mama. I am sorry all this has happened to you." I seemed to be spending more and more time apologizing lately. "How about I get you a fresh cup of tea, and then we can talk." My gosh, that kettle was getting a workout! If Papa ever managed to get the plumbing working, the next thing I would ask for would be an electric stove. This was just ridiculous!

The sky had gone dark and I closed the curtains. I turned on the bedside lamp, and Irene sat there with Edith while I went to fix the tea. I figured I could stall for time if I played it right. I still needed to have a conversation with Auntie. There never seemed to be time. Perhaps tonight, when everyone was tucked in, we could be alone and I could get answers to at least some of these crazy questions. As I waited for the water to come to a boil, I took a closer look at Mama's bracelet.

Irish Mist

It looked old. Old in the sense that it came from the old world, a time when stories of Irish healers abounded. I could remember Mama telling us the stories that her mother had told her when she was a girl. The bracelet was truly beautiful. It looked like it was made of fine Irish silver. There were three charms hanging on the rope chain. A Celtic Knot, an Irish Rose, and an Owl. An Owl? Now I had more questions for my getting-longer-by-the-minute list.

Auntie, who apparently was in the kitchen with me now, looked over my shoulder at the bracelet and said quietly, her voice heavy with sadness, "I bought that for her. It was meant to be her birthday gift that year. I never got the chance to see her put it on. It must have been found in my things after I was gone. I had it all wrapped up in pretty paper and ribbons, with her name on it, for her special day."

#20 Pillow Talk

Mama was settled in for the night, Papa had come inside, and one by one the lights were turned off and the old farmhouse settled into darkness. The wind picked up and dried the rain-soaked leaves, tossing them in the air in clumps of composting fibre. The branches of the tall tamarack that grew under the roof eave of my bedroom pressed against the faded blue board-and-batten siding of the house and made odd scraping noises. It had been a very long day. Thank goodness, Mama was home. I had the feeling that things were going to be all right now, despite the crazy chain of events over the last several days. I mulled them over

Chapter 1 - The Well

as I gave my long auburn hair a good brushing. Didn't seem that I'd had much time for such vanity lately. As I pulled the horsehair bristles through my knots, I remembered the Celtic knots on the bracelet. I looked over to my bed, and there, relaxed and comfy with her head on my pile of pillows, was Aunt Irene. She was so pretty. People said I looked like her. I didn't see it, but then when had I ever had the opportunity? I had only been a wee child when she had left us.

"Now's the time," she smiled. "Ask away!"

For all the waiting that Colleen had done for this moment to arrive, she didn't know where to start. She considered it briefly and then jumped in with the idea that if you had no idea of where to start, then, quite simply, start at the beginning. "Auntie," she began, "how did you come to be in the well?"

Irene began the story with the day of the accident. "It was the rushing water that took the car downstream. I remember how it poured in the window, frigid cold and frightful. I couldn't move, perhaps I had hit my head—I don't know. That is all I can remember. It was the same with the well, frigid cold and oh, so frightful to be stuck in there. I waited for you. It took so long. You had to make the wish to set me free. The wish about your brother. It was he who had kept me trapped. All those years lost to his childlike feelings. He thought he had control, he thought it was all about him. He had cursed himself and me with that thinking because he wouldn't let go of a responsibility that was not his

Irish Mist

to hold. Colleen, you hold the spirit of generosity and compassion, of love and encouragement. That is what set him free and freed me as well. That day—the wish you made for him—I know you were frustrated in your thinking. The need for him to smarten up came from deeper in your heart. You wanted happiness for him even though you had not a clue about what had taken it from him in the first place."

Colleen stared at her aunt. The wind howled and the shadows filled the corners of her bedroom. The wallpaper looked silly now, almost childish. She felt older. The wisdom of another world was slowly filling her being, just as her aunt had done, only a few days before. She looked again at the bracelet with its three charms. "Auntie, tell me about the charms. Why did you choose those?"

"The Sisters Knot heart was for Edith and me and our sister who died from the poliovirus. Her name was Maeve and she was the eldest. Edith is the only one left who walks this earth. The heart is a symbol of sisterhood and the strong, eternal bond that we share. See how the shape is made in one unbroken line? The triple spiral, woven in its middle, is for the three stages of woman: the maid, the mother, and the wise woman." Irene rolled over onto her side to face her niece, and the bracelet fell away from Colleen's wrist. She looked at it with eyes that saw into the past. "The next one here is the Wild Irish Rose. This untameable, sweet briar survives in the wildest and harshest of habitats." She smiled at the thought of the fiery spirit that she saw so clearly in Colleen.

Chapter 1 - The Well

"Now we come to the last, the Owl. The Owl is a creature of keen sight in darkness. Celtic folklore says the wise Owl can give you wisdom by helping unmask those who would deceive you. And that can include your own self!" Irene paused again, knowing that this was a lot to take in. "It was these three that I thought Edith should have. If I had been alive, I would have added another each year. It would be quite the weight by now!" They both had a giggle over that one.

Colleen turned out the light and snatched one of the pillows from under her aunt's head. They lay beside each other in the darkness. The moon broke through the clouds and shone brightly in the wide Saskatchewan sky. The stars twinkled with vibrant energy as the answers unfolded, and ever so gently, found their place in Colleen's mind.

#21 The Family Business

Arthur Cadwyn Timmons was born in rural Saskatchewan in 1920. His father had been a carpenter, born in Ireland, and his mother was from Wales. They had emigrated separately and met in post-war Canada at a church social. Arthur was the eldest of their four children. He had two brothers, twins, and a sister. His brothers had not had an easy life and had died young, during the 1951 influenza epidemic. Most of his siblings had moved to western Canada, but Arthur felt that Saskatchewan was home and he had never left: that is, until he signed up to serve in the armed forces during the Second World War. Gladys, his sister, still lived in Saskatoon with her husband. Their

Irish Mist

son, Darryl, now living in North Dakota, was Arthur's nephew and Gladys' only child. He was the one who sent packages to his uncle each month.

In 1941, Arthur had been of age to enter the war. He was young and strong and ready to go. He originally signed on as an infantryman but in 1945 became involved in the building of mobile army surgical units because of his carpentry skills. It was then that he was injured. A bad fall had left him disabled, and he received a medical discharge. He returned home, dependent on narcotics for pain management.

Arthur married Edith Colleen McNab in the Anglican Church on Main Street in Back of Beyond, Saskatchewan in the fall of 1947. They moved in with Edith's parents on the McNab family farm and two years later, Andy was born. Three years later, he was followed by his brother, Colby, and then Colleen in 1954. Times were hard for the young Timmons family. Arthur only had a veteran's disability pension, and once Edith became pregnant, she was no longer welcome in the working world. Arthur's parents had already passed on, and the small inheritance had been shared among the four siblings. Arthur did what he could to help on the farm, driving the tractor and doing repairs. When Irene, Edith's sister, came up with the idea of producing methamphetamines, it sounded like an answer to all their problems. The ingredients were easily obtained, there were no laws in place to stop them, and they lived in the middle of nowhere. It was perfect. Right up until Irene had died.

Chapter 1 - The Well

Ten years later, here he was, in the far-back shed, mixing and blending and doing what he had been doing for years. Irene had been the brains behind everything. She had organized and instructed. She was the one who had run interference when it was needed. Now it had fallen to him. Was there never an end to this? He had made such a mess of things. He had failed miserably, despite having been able to kick his own habit. It was still hard some days: the pain got to him and he resorted to the whiskey bottle for medicinal purposes.

The thought of what his current occupation was doing to others was something he could not consider. He would not be able to continue if he spent a moment thinking about it. His livelihood would be lost.

He hated that he was dependent on his family for supply deliveries and drug running. He didn't want to do it any more. He was tired. Tired of all the stress, tired of all the subterfuge. Tired of dodging questions and making up answers. He just needed to be able to relax and enjoy life a bit more, put his feet up, maybe take a trip somewhere, see a bit of the country, or visit with his brothers out west. He wanted to stop worrying about every dollar. Edith deserved a furnace and a bathroom. The kids deserved an education. He didn't want them to be tied to the family business. They should have their own lives, be able to see their dreams come true without the constraints of the dark side and the evil it perpetrated.

Arthur decided that he needed a break from all this thinking. He should drive over to Sybil Bisbee's on the weekend. A pint of ale with some of his cronies would always brighten things up.

Andy was at a crossroad. He had completed the initial recruitment process, filling out forms and making appointments for hearing and vision tests. He didn't think that there would be any difficulties with the physical fitness aspect of it as he had been a farm boy all his life. The stumbling block came in the section regarding questions about "being of good character." He thought of himself as kind and considerate. He had been raised in a Christian community. That had to count for something. He had a friend who was an officer and would vouch for him. But there was a wee problem with the family business. On paper it all looked good. Ma took care of that. However, anyone poking their nose deeper would surely notice the something-else-going-on that had been going on for a very long time. He decided that before he went any further, he was going to have an honest chat with his father. The corner table of Sybil Bisbee's would work, maybe this weekend, but definitely sooner than later.

#22 Wednesday

The rooster crowed in his usual boisterous manner as the early morning sun shot orange arrows into the eastern sky. Colleen opened her eyes reluctantly. It had been a late night of thinking and rethinking for her. The silver bracelet with its intricate charms lay on the

Chapter 1 - The Well

pillow beside her. She picked it up in her hand, holding it tight until she had it secured in the front pocket of her jeans. She tied back her hair with a rubber elastic, shoved her feet with their thick wool socks into a pair of clogs, and went down the stairs to the kitchen. The woodbox had been left empty last night, and she had neither the time nor inclination to fill it now. As she turned on the two-burner hotplate, she knew she would get heck for doing it. Papa always said it was too much money to be paying out for electricity when there was plenty of wood to burn for free. Well, damn it, there was no wood to be seen right now. *Someone* had forgotten to fill the bin. *Was that going to be her job now?* She pumped water with extra energy, filled the blasted kettle, and stomped off to get wood. The kitchen was too cold to sit in.

When Colleen hauled the armload of wood into the house, the kettle was boiling furiously on the hotplate. She poured water onto the teabags and set the pot of breakfast oatmeal on the still-hot burner to cook. The Owl charm, digging into her hip, sent a silent reminder. Mama would be so happy to have her bracelet back. Irene, as though summoned, appeared behind her, and Colleen almost collided with her aunt as she turned to set the table. The ever-cheery Irene bid her a good morning. "Let's go," she said. "I can't wait for Edith to see me!"

"Huh?" Colleen asked. "What do you mean 'see you'?"

"Well," she explained, "If she has the bracelet, then won't she be able to see me?"

Irish Mist

"She had the bracelet before and couldn't see you. Why would now be different?"

"Ah," she countered, "that was before. I was still trapped in the well then. See, it's like this. You found me, you made your lovely wish, Andy let go of his guilt, and now I am free. When Edith puts her bracelet back on, then the three of us will be together. It is you and I who share the mind, but the power of the Owl will let its wearer see my spirit."

The oatmeal threatened to boil over the side of the pot.

In the city, Andy was getting a head start on stocking the shelves at the grocery store. He was looking at 26 weeks' worth of training at the RCMP facility in Regina if things worked out that way, and he would have to quit his job. As he worked, he thought about the conversation he would have with his father. He was hoping that it would go well. He just wasn't quite sure what to say.

Colb was seated in the classroom at school, daydreaming about the pretty girl in the post office, Mrs. Kovetski's daughter. He was almost at the end of semester. Soon he would be starting his placement for the summer at the co-op, just two miles from home. He would volunteer to make a run to the post office every day if he could manage it. Ma's birthday was coming up soon. Maybe Marsha Kovetski could help him pick out something for her. He was no good at

Chapter 1 - The Well

that sort of thing. The sound of his teacher clearing his throat brought Colb back to the here and now.

Arthur rose from his bed, giving Edith a quick kiss on the uninjured side of her forehead. He dropped his pyjamas on the floor and put on clean underwear and socks from his drawer. His pants and shirt from yesterday were hanging on the hook fastened to the side of his highboy dresser, and he dressed quickly. The cows were waiting. It was the best part of his day. He loved the calmness of the barn and the sweet smell of hay. He was at peace with his bovine companions. They held no judgment over him.

Once Arthur was done with the milking and had had his tea, he drove into town and parked in front of the post office. He handed his notice-of-delivery slip to Mrs. Kovetski. She reached behind her, sorted through the pile of items on the long counter, and handed him a brown envelope. Same as usual. No problem today. He walked over to the co-op and rummaged through the plumbing supplies until he found what he needed, paid for his purchase, got back in the truck, and headed for home. Halfway there he remembered Edith's birthday. He turned the truck around and went back to town.

Edith awoke with the same blaring headache that she had had every day since Saturday. She struggled to her feet, at the same time realizing that the chamber pot was not going to be an easy option for her. She sat back down and called for her daughter. She called again, louder this time. When Colleen still did not

Irish Mist

respond, Edith felt her only choice was to brave the pain in her head and she reached for the chamber pot, cursing her husband and his lack of initiative when it came to indoor plumbing. She would have to find a way to get him moving on that.

Colleen went down the hall towards the bedroom with the tea things, Irene following at her heels. Mama was balancing precariously on the chamber pot when the two of them walked into the room.

#23 A Blend of Irish Mist

Finally, the three of us were together, like the three charms of the bracelet. Mama, the Sister, Irene, the Owl, and me, Colleen, the Rose. It was quite the scene. Mama had her knickers down, Irene was somewhere in between seen and unseen, and I was almost hopping up and down with excitement. I helped get the knickers up and relocated the half-filled chamber pot to its spot under the bed frame. I hoped I wouldn't forget it was there.

"Mama, I have your bracelet. Papa brought it home from the hospital for you. He was afraid it might get nicked by some unsavoury character while you were asleep. I'm sure you've been missing it. Let me put it on your wrist." I leaned over and fastened the clasp for her, stole a sideways glance at Auntie, and held my breath. I waited. Irene waited. Nothing happened.

"Colleen, thank you! I have missed it. You know, your Aunt Irene would have given this to me ten years

Chapter 1 - The Well

ago this weekend. She died the day before my birthday. It was so very sad. You remember her, don't you? Papa found this bracelet with her things. I guess he was looking for papers or other stuff, and he came upon this little box, all wrapped up nice and with my name on it. When he brought it home to me, I couldn't stop crying. She was the only sister I had left, and she was gone now too. She was so kind, always with a smile and something good to say. She found special meaning in things. I can't help but wonder about the charms. She would have picked them out herself. They must mean something that only she could explain. I wish I could ask her; I wish that we could have time together again."

As Mama spoke the words, I watched Irene change form. She turned from the beautiful young woman with slender shoulders and an auburn mane of hair that fell almost to her waist, into a mist. The mist from the well. She swirled in the air and wrapped herself around Mama like a cashmere shawl. Warm and soft and comforting. Mama's face erupted in joy as she stroked the shawl, feeling it hug her, feeling the love of her sister. I felt that I had just witnessed a miracle, something that could not be explained or explained away. It was the most beautiful thing I had ever seen.

I sat down on the other side of the bed and listened as Irene told her sister the story of the charms and their meaning. I left shortly after that to look after the endless chore list that, of late, seemed to follow me all day. Edith and Irene spent the rest of the morning together. There was lots to talk about. I felt happy for them and for me as well. This was a whole new

Irish Mist

beginning, and I was delighted to be part of it. I felt a connection that had never been there before. Good things would surely follow.

Papa returned from town with his usual collection of bags and packages. I noticed the brown envelope that he had picked up from the post office. It probably was from my cousin Darryl. He was also carrying a long length of copper pipe and various plumbing pieces. *Was he really was going to turn on the water to the bathroom?* This was cause for celebration. Men just didn't understand how important these things were to women. But I was truly glad that, for whatever reason, he had decided that it was important today. Perhaps I would try my hand at baking a cake! We could have a birthday party, and there would be a very special guest at this one.

Before I could get going with that thought, the phone rang. We had a party line, which meant that we had our own ring, two long and one short. We shared the line with the Henckels next door and the Schmidts, next to them. The Schmidts owned the bakery in town. Sometimes Papa would bring home treats from their shop in white cardboard boxes that they tied with string. If he came in the door with any of those, we all knew he had just been paid for selling something. All of a sudden it occurred to me that I had never wondered what that might have been. I guess that I was too interested in the contents of the box—gugelhupf and streusel, sometimes squares of carrot cake or poppy seed filled pastries—to give it

Chapter 1 - The Well

more thought. You could tell just by looking at Mrs. Schmidt that she was an excellent baker!

I ran for the phone, almost tripping over the cat! *How did she get in again?* I hoped she was pregnant. Kittens were so much fun. I heard Andy's voice on the other end. It was not his usual monotone. He sounded happy. He and Colb would be coming Thursday night. They both had Friday off, and they thought they would drive up from the city when they were done for the day. They would be staying for the weekend, maybe longer. Andy rattled on, reminding me that it was Ma's birthday and asking if my airhead brain had remembered that. He asked if I could ready the upstairs bedroom for them—make up the beds and stuff like that. He held back from giving me any further details, then with a quick, "see you tomorrow night," he hung up. Well! I was beyond excited. I danced my way through the rest of the day.

#24 Thursday

Thursday was a busy day. There was so much to do. Thankfully, the weather cooperated, with sun and clouds and a wind from the west that didn't threaten to steal the sheets from the clothesline. The washing got done in the morning with the use of the wringer washer that was kept next to the freezer in the storage shed. I hung the laundry on the line to dry in the spring breeze. Later this afternoon, the beds could be made up with fresh linens for the boys. Papa was working on the water lines to the bathroom. They would be connected before long. That was the report coming from under the house in Papa's muffled voice.

In the early afternoon, Mama was feeling much better and sat in the kitchen, helping to cut vegetables for the soup that would soon be simmering on the stove. It should go nicely with some loaves of crusty bread from Mrs. Schmidt's bakery. Papa had given in to my plea for store-bought bread since he was going to town anyway. He thought he had all the plumbing bits necessary, but had to go back to the co-op for something else. It seems he had decided to repair the hot water tank that was attached to the side of the wood stove. More good things to come. He was full of surprises lately.

When Papa left for town, it was easy for the three of us to talk uninterrupted. We went back and forth about anything that came to mind, easy and fun conversation that had us all laughing. It seemed so normal, not a bit of the unusual going on. *How could that be?* I stood at the stove, scraping carrots from the cutting board into the soup pot while I watched the two sisters chatting over a cup of tea. Well, one cup of tea. It seems that Auntie hadn't yet gotten the hang of moving solid objects with her hands. She had had a few spills. She claimed that she would manage that in time, all things going as planned. Mama pointed out that Irene had always been the planner of the family. They looked at each other in an odd way. The conversation moved on rather abruptly, I thought. I was starting to pick up on a lot of things but saw no reason to start asking questions just then. I had done

Chapter 1 - The Well

enough of that lately. The giggling resumed as they talked about silly stuff, about housekeeping and fancy dresses, and discussing the ways of the world and the ways to cook a chicken. It made my heart sing.

Andy and Colb arrived around nine in the evening. They were tired from their day of work, school, and the drive from the city. They grabbed a sandwich and a glass of milk, toted their duffel bags up the stairs, and went to sleep. I wondered if they even noticed the outdoorsy smell of line-dried sheets. When the kitchen looked clean and Mama was tucked in, I went to bed too. Maybe I could read my book for a bit. Mama was getting better, and I would be back to school next week. I would probably have a ton of homework. The library book would be coming due for return, and I had hardly spent any time reading.

Through my window, I could see the light on in the far-back shed. Papa was wearing that weird mask, busy mixing whatever it was that he felt the need to be mixing at that late hour. I was more tired than I had realized, and the book fell from my fingers, the light from the bedside lamp still glowing.

#25 Bisbee's on Back Street

Friday morning brought more rain to the prairies. Sodden leaves covered the ground, and the smell of fresh earth and wet dog overpowered anything produced on the stove for breakfast. I sprinkled more cinnamon on the boiling oats. I put the jug of maple syrup and a bowl of dried fruit on the table to make things a bit more cheery. Papa had let the dogs in when he left for the barn, and they lay on the pine plank floor thumping their soggy tails, hoping for sloppy eaters. No one was going to give him heck about the dogs, but I got yelled at for a cat sneaking in! Life was not fair.

The day moved along with routine chores. Mama was looking more spry and was delighted to be able to use the indoor privy. *Will hot water be next?* Around teatime the men came inside, shaking the rainwater from their outdoor clothing and bringing spring mud in on their boots. Papa said not to hold supper for them: they were going to change their clothes so as they didn't smell like a barn and head into town. They were going to stop in at the Bisbee's and have a chat with Ray Bisbee about maybe getting Colb some part-time work. Ray's wife had been feeling poorly of late, and he was having to lend a hand at the house. He needed extra help in the shop. They might stay a bit longer and say hello to whatever folks might be visiting with his wife, Sybil, when they were done with their business with Ray.

The Bisbees owned a large piece of land within the town perimeter, facing on Back Street. There was a wide gravel driveway that ran from the street to the house and then around to the steel barn-type structure in the rear of the property. That was where Ray had his Small Engine & Appliance Repair shop. It smelled of rust and dust and motor oil. The pegboard walls were covered with an assortment of tools, ropes, drive belts, and air hoses, all hanging at odd angles from metal hooks. The floor was concrete, but you could hardly

Chapter 1 - The Well

see that. Scattered about were lawn mowers and tillers, chain saws and water pumps, all of them interspersed with vacuum cleaners and floor polishers. He had a lot of vacuum cleaners. Cone shaped hair dryers, toasters and Sunbeam Mixmasters, in some state of repair, or disrepair, sat on makeshift wood tables. Discarded lengths of wire and misplaced screwdrivers decorated any remaining surfaces. Ray did it all, or at least he tried to.

Sybil had many years ago gotten him to build a large sunroom off the main kitchen. It was furnished with small tables and ladder-back chairs, an Acorn stove for heat, and large windows that let in the sun when it was shining. Soon, either the end of April or early May, the removable storm windows that kept out the cold and wind would be replaced with the screens that kept out the mosquitoes and flies. Sybil liked to "entertain," and there were always a few people sitting around enjoying drinks and conversation. She kept a stock of bagged potato chips, pretzels, and portions of salted nuts in the upper glass-fronted cupboards of an old pine Hoosier at the back of the room. On its porcelain countertop was an assortment of teabags and a jar of instant coffee for the group that came in after the Tuesday evening meeting in the church basement. The Maxwell House coffee can was for "donations," should anyone be so inclined. Sometimes she offered pickled eggs, crammed together in a large Mason jar. They were 10 cents each. There was no sign announcing that, people just knew. Beside the pine cabinet was the largest refrigerator that the Sears Catalogue offered, and it took up the remaining wall space.

Irish Mist

Aunt Irene had told me about Sybil's sunroom. Seems that Sybil had been "entertaining" for a very long time. No one complained, and she continued to provide a place for locals to socialize while her husband maintained a thriving business. Aunt Irene had told me about a lot of things in the last few days. I was getting a whole new type of education while I was off school, taking care of women's work.

At the repair shop, Ray was busy balancing a newly sharpened lawn mower blade. He stood up and nodded to each of the boys as Arthur introduced them. Colb looked around him at the disorder of the shop. He was just itching to put things where he thought they should be. His mouth kicked into gear, and he blurted out, "Mr. Bisbee, sir, can I just move the vacuum cleaners into the space under the hoses? If you men are going to be chatting here, then I could have that done for you in a few minutes. It wouldn't be any trouble."

Ray turned his attention to Colb. "I didn't know you were looking for work, but if you like, you might have yourself a job. You can start now and show me what you can do." He wiped his hands on the rag he produced from the back pocket of his overalls. He shifted his eyes to Arthur. "How about we go up to the house and have a beer? Andy, will you join us?" They left Colb to his fun, and the three of them walked across the driveway to the house.

Chapter 1 - The Well

#26 Man Plans While God Laughs

It was late in the day, and the clearing clouds gave way to a few streaks of fading light. The men helped themselves to bottles of ale from the enormous refrigerator and dropped the appropriate amount of cash in the coffee can on the counter. Andy, always hungry, grabbed himself a bag of chips and dug in his pocket for change, dropping it into the can, where it made clinking sounds as it hit the bottom. Ray helped himself to a pickled egg from the Mason jar and a handful of soda crackers from the wicker basket beside the eggs.

The conversation started in earnest when they sat down at a corner table, away from the rest of Sybil's "guests." There was no point in having their conversation overheard. People in small towns had their own way of entertaining themselves, and it often had to do with the spreading of gossip. Simply, it was just something to do. Ray lowered his voice. He knew all about the family business, and he had helped out on more than one occasion by storing product that was between seller and buyer. No reason to advertise that fact.

Between bites and chewing, Andy relayed his plan for his future. He took a few quick swigs of his ale to clear his mouth of food and give him a bit of liquid courage. "I can't do it no more," he said. "This is something I really want, and I can't be in law enforcement and running drugs for you at the same time. I have to be out." He took another drink from his almost empty bottle. "Could you not find something else to do that would make money? Alcohol is legal.

Irish Mist

Why not produce that? Ma has been making hooch for years. Put a label on it and get a licence. How about something like 'Timmons Toddy'?"

Ray and Arthur thought that maybe the young man had a good idea. Ray got up and walked to the fridge to get another round of the strong, amber-coloured ale. "Colb can drive you guys home when we're done. Let's make a plan."

At the farmhouse, the hearty soup simmered on the stove. Edith and Colleen, with Irene's help, worked together to make a plan for a party on Saturday evening. It was short notice but a bit of fun would be good. Edith wasn't calling it a birthday party because she didn't want or need any more presents. The gift of her long-dead sister in her life was more than enough. It was too bad that Irene's surprise appearance was something she could not share with her guests.

Phone calls were made to several of the neighbours, inviting them to bring salads or desserts, along with whatever they might like to drink and, of course, folding chairs. Edith would be supplying the main course and the cake. Along with the cake, she planned to share some of her most excellent dessert whiskey from the oak cask that had aged the longest. She had her own special recipe. It had been passed down to her from her mother who had been making backyard booze since the time of prohibition!

Edith had changed the original recipe a bit, adding some specific ingredients that she had been able to

Chapter 1 - The Well

find locally. They had plants in the wetlands that grew nowhere else, and the bees harvested the pollen to produce a honey with a unique taste. Her finished product was even more pleasing to the palate than her mother's offerings had been. Colleen ran off to the freezer to get out a large roast for the meal. Edith sorted through her recipe box looking for the index card with instructions for the cake she wanted to make. Irene danced about the room in her swirling-mist way, offering up suggestions and making comments. Such fun she had not had in a very long time!

#27 Colby Mathias Timmons

Colby Mathias Timmons would be seventeen on his next birthday, which was still six months away. He had been born in the fall, just as the first of the snow had laid its blanket on the ground. His mother had a liking for the letter M, probably her contribution to the child-naming process from her maiden name of McNab. Mathias wasn't such a bad choice for a middle name, and Malachi, Andy's middle name was great, as far as he was concerned. It was poor Colleen that he felt for. When Mama was mad, she yelled out his sister's full name at high volume. "Colleen Muriel Timmons! Where is your head? What were you thinking?" It always started off with something like that. Probably because Colleen hadn't been thinking, again. It was truly a blessing that she was such an airhead because he hardly ever got blamed for stuff.

Colby had been taking things apart for as long as he could remember: radios and toasters and anything

75

Irish Mist

else he could take a screwdriver to. He had learned that appliances needed to be unplugged beforehand the hard way. That is what he had been told—he didn't remember that part.

Colb got busy as soon as the men left for the house. He knew that he would have lots of time to rearrange the contents of the shop. A beer in the house was never just one beer. There was always a second round, sometimes a third. Then he would get to drive the truck home, something he had been doing long before he had a driver's licence. He guessed that Ray hadn't recognized him. He had grown about a foot taller in the six months that he had been away at school in the city. He had to shave almost every day now too. He wondered if Marsha Kovetski would be as impressed with that development as he was. If Ray took too long getting back, then Colb figured he could make himself indispensable because his new boss would need lots of help to find things.

It turned out that Colb was completely accurate with his prediction of the timing of things. It was quite a while later before Arthur and Andy signalled him from the sunroom door. They were ready to head for home. Ray tossed his set of keys across the driveway and yelled for Colb to set the padlock on the steel door: he was done with work for the day. When Colb brought him back the key ring, Ray said, "Thanks, lad. Come back and see me on Monday morning, and we'll talk about making you an employee. It's hard to find young people who are interested in getting their hands dirty. I think you will work out just fine." He

Chapter 1 - The Well

gave Colb a hearty slap on the back and went inside to finish his waiting beer.

When they got home, the boys helped themselves to the pot of soup and crusty bread, spread thick with butter, and big hunks of goat cheese. They always had an appetite. Arthur was deep in thought and stirred his spoon around in his bowl for a while before he finally ate the rest of his meal. Mama made a pot of tea, and the family sat around and talked in front of the fire until it got late. The three kids went upstairs, Mama was tidying up the last of the tea things, and Papa went out to the far-back shed. He said he had some tidying up to do as well.

Arthur walked to the back of his property through the soon-to-be-planted cornfield and opened the padlock to his shed. It was chilly inside, and he plugged in the space heater, thinking he should get a new one soon; the on/off switch hadn't worked worth a damn in years. He turned on the radio to a music station and started moving jugs around aimlessly. He didn't know what the answer was. He had been doing this for so long, he didn't know any other way. What the hell was he supposed to do? Andy was right to want to get out. He couldn't put his kids at risk. Their future was more important than anything. He hated the thought of asking Colb to drive for him. He couldn't do it, he just couldn't. He leaned against the old warped countertop and made his decision. He turned off the radio, secured the padlock, and walked back to the house, feeling vulnerable and relieved at the same time. If he had been a praying man, he would have been on his knees.

Irish Mist

Colleen picked up her book and read another chapter. She could hear her brothers talking quietly to each other in the next room. She saw the light go out in the far-back shed. She said good night to Auntie and turned out her light. Tomorrow was Mama's birthday.

#28 Edith's 45th Birthday

Saturday was going to be a great day. Colleen could feel it. She was up with the rooster and had breakfast ready to go on the table in record time. The hot water tank that was attached to the wood stove seemed like it actually might produce hot water in the near future. The indoor privy was working well, her brothers were home, and Mama was up and about again. Colleen thought she might have seen a smile on her father's all too serious face yesterday.

There was much to be done before the neighbours arrived this afternoon, and she focused herself on the tasks at hand. Mama was measuring flour into a mixing bowl and humming to herself as she moved about the rustic kitchen. Andy and Colb had gone to town, no doubt shopping for a last minute birthday gift for their mother. Papa was busy outside: there had been a fox roving around, and he was securing fencing. The sheep would be ready for shearing in a week or so, and he had stuff to do around that as well. Colleen had been so busy; she didn't think she'd seen Aunt Irene all day. Maybe she had been keeping Mama company.

Finally everything was done. Mama went into her bedroom to put on a pretty dress. Papa followed her

Chapter 1 - The Well

down the hall and Colleen heard the bedroom door close softly. She knew what all that giggling meant. Could be that was why Irene was suddenly standing beside her. "Hi," she said. "Everything ready? I'm so excited. I wish I could have drinks and cake too!" It seemed strange to hear Auntie being the one making wishes.

The neighbours started arriving around four, bringing all sorts of delicious-looking dishes. The sideboard quickly filled up with serving bowls and bottles of different shapes and sizes. There was lots of talking and laughing, with everyone enjoying the impromptu gathering. When the food was heated up and ready to eat, Papa thought it appropriate to say Grace. As soon as he said Amen, Ron Henckel suggested that they all acknowledge the special reason for the party. Mama blushed prettily and smiled her consent.

As the guests raised their glasses in a toast to Edith's 45th birthday, the house shook from its foundation to the top of its steel roof, the windows rattled in their frames, and a deafening blast came from the direction of the far-back shed.

All conversation stopped. The Henckel boys started to giggle. Mr. and Mrs. Henckel looked at each other with an expression of well-that-ain't-no-surprise on their faces. The Schmidts tried to cover their embarrassment. It was such an outrage to have neighbours engaged in nefarious activity.

Irish Mist

Edith shot a questioning glare at Arthur. Arthur shrugged his shoulders, an I-don't-know expression on his face. That changed very quickly, as the light bulb turned on in his brain. He bellowed out a very loud, "Ah! Damn!" and followed that up with a much quieter, "I forgot to unplug the space heater."

Andy recognized the sound of an exploding meth lab and said to himself and anyone who might hear him in the crowded room, "Well, I guess that settles that!"

Colb had a pretty good idea of what had just happened. He looked out the window, saw that it was indeed the far-back shed that had gone up in a blaze, and rued the loss of his stash of weed. It had been in a coffee can under the bench, behind the containers of paint thinner.

Colleen had been trying to sneak a shot of Mama's prized hooch when the shed blew up. She had figured everyone was occupied with toasting the birthday girl, and it would be the perfect opportunity. She dropped her glass before she had managed a sip, and it smashed on the floor. No one heard the crash.

Irene had been working the crowd, flowing around the room like the happy ghost she was. When the house started shaking and the rocking chairs started rocking, she yelled out, "Whoo Hoo! Isn't this a party! Happy Birthday, Edith!" No one heard her either.

Chapter 1 - The Well

#29 Timmons Toddy

The far-back shed had been built by the creek a very long time ago, but Papa, surprisingly, had kept it in good repair, the exception to that being the old space heater with its broken switch. It was called the far-back shed for good reason. It was as far back from the house and the other outbuildings as possible. The thawed ground was saturated with spring moisture and the fire would not spread past its immediate perimeter. As a result, the flames self-extinguished, and the party continued with only a minor interruption. The talk in the room turned to the subject of insurance claims, deductibles, and how those people were all a bunch of thieves and you never really got your money's worth. Colleen got out the dustpan and hastily cleaned up the broken shards before anyone could accuse her of wrongdoing. The guests refilled their glasses, Edith cut the cake, and Andy and Colb went around the room passing out plates of dessert, plastic forks, and paper napkins.

Hours later, when everyone left for home, Mama got to open her gifts from us. Papa presented her with a Sears gift certificate in a fancy envelope. Andy and Colb had chipped in together and bought her a new hand mixer. Aunt Irene had found a way to order a new charm for Mama's bracelet, but it wouldn't be at the post office for another week. I asked Colb to pick up the package when it came in, giving him an excuse for a visit with Marsha Kovetski. I went last and handed Mama the shawl I had made for her. I had been working on it since Christmas. The yarn was a

Irish Mist

light blue, her favourite colour. It was full of mistakes and the sides didn't match up, but she said she loved it and wrapped its warmth around her shoulders.

We all went to church the next morning, squished into the truck like the close family we were. The plaster strips on Mama's forehead had fallen off, and the gash no longer looked quite so bad. We had things to be thankful for, lots of things. We also had a few things to say sorry for. So much had happened in just a week's time.

On Monday morning, Mrs. Jansen waited at the road, the school bus idling as usual. As I ran down the driveway, I could tell that she was happy to see me. There was a big smile on her friendly face. She had heard about Mama's accident and expressed concern for her quick return to health. The ladies had missed her being at the bridge club on Thursday afternoon.

Andy phoned the recruitment centre in Regina and inquired about the status of his application. He was ready to move forward with his life. He was more than pleased when it was Miss Byrne-Calder who had answered the telephone.

Colb started his new job at Ray's Small Engine and Appliance Repair and would be there full time until he began his four hours per day placement at the co-op.

Papa was busy as always, with sheep and cows and fences. When he came inside for his dinner at noon, there was lots of talk about the old whiskey recipe,

Chapter 1 - The Well

trademarks, and licence applications. It looked like there was to be a new family business, one that we could all be proud of. Timmons Toddy. What a great idea!

Irene was more than delighted that, by the simple wish of a child, a whole family had been set free from its bonds of grief and tragedy. She set about making plans and organizing her thoughts for the new endeavour.

Edith dreamed of a new furnace as she smiled to herself. She had a secret.

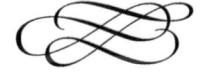

Irish Mist

Chapter 2
The Boy on the Rock

My Roots

On March 31, 1949, Newfoundland and Labrador joined Canada and became its tenth province. In 1949, on March 31, Margaret Roisin (Ro-sheen) Calder gave birth to a scrawny, squalling, infant girl. That was me. It was more than luck that brought me into the world. The labour was long and complicated: the midwife almost lost mother and child. While the expectant father paced nervously on the porch, Gramma Byrne, Margaret's mother, pushed her way past him with a look of fierce determination on her face and a trail of no nonsense in her frothy wake. It's never been told exactly what it was that Gramma B did to make things happen, but she rarely depended on luck. In short order the sounds of new life were heard, clear out to the chicken coop. It was apparent that I, Maisie Roisin Frances Byrne-Calder, wanted the world to know that I had arrived. Graeme Calder, my Da, stopped his pacing and moved his feet to the rhythm of the Scottish jig that he often heard playing in his head when he was happy. He had no idea what the name of the tune was, but he had loved the sound of the fiddle since he was a child. *T'was a fine tune indeed, to match a fine day.*

The Calders were a blended family, if such a thing was given a name in 1949. Blended meant, quite simply, that we were a mixed bunch: Irish and Scottish, Protestant and Catholic. Graeme Calder came from a family of proud and rugged Scots, transplanted from the highlands after the Great Depression. He had six brothers and two sisters, not as large a family as some, but large enough that he understood the pains of an empty belly and the harshness of life. Margaret, my Ma, was born a Byrne. She had been carried in her mother's womb aboard the ship that had brought her parents to the new land many years past. Brigid and Colin Byrne were Irish, from the southern area near the shores of County Cork. When Margaret birthed Maisie, the child brought the light of hope into the world for them once again. It had been a difficult year.

Gramma B, as the locals called her, was a woman of spirit and wisdom. There wasn't much worth knowing that she didn't already know. But she was always willing to learn: there were things in this new world she had not seen before. When she was a child, she had been taught about the Irish healers, how their wisdom was passed down through the generations of family. Her growing up had been hard, a time of hunger and disease, of war and suffering.

Chapter 2 - The Boy on the Rock

Brigid Byrne, or Gram as I called her, hoped that her home in Newfoundland would be a change from that, and in some ways it was. The landscape was similar, deep inlets and rocky escarpments, bogs and marshland, blue sky and blue sea, timbered mountains and fast-running streams. The Ireland that she loved could be seen all around her, providing the warm hug of familiarity. What she hoped would be absent was the war of religious wills, the agony of the past and angst of the future, and the grimness of reality. This new start held promise of better days ahead. The Beothuk and the Mi'kmaq had survived for hundreds of years on The Rock: the Celts would do no worse.

Maisie Roisin Frances Byrne-Calder

Eight years later, I was no longer a squalling infant, or even scrawny. I had grown tall. To this day, I still have the beautiful chestnut curls that won't be tamed and the attitude to match. Gram said I was precocious. I probably still am. Maisie Roisin Frances Byrne-Calder is quite the name for a child. When my mother was annoyed with me, it took a long while for her to list all of my names in proper order. I started to run after I heard the first two called out—no need to be waiting for more. There were lots of places to hide if I didn't want to be found. I disliked chores. The cleaning of fish was gross. The beating of carpets made me sneeze. I much preferred to spend my days, the warm and sunny ones, running along the shore chasing sea birds or lying on the grass counting clouds. I loved to watch the humpback whales when they appeared in spring and summer. They slapped their enormous flukes against the sea and sang

Irish Mist

their song as they went by. I knew that they talked to each other. Not like people talk, but I had heard them. I wished I could understand their conversations and as I watched them play in the blue waves, I imagined what they might be talking about. They probably didn't exchange recipes for jam or preserves like women pushing baby carriages, but I'll bet they did tell each other where the best krill or cod might be. Perhaps they discussed family issues, misbehaving offspring or troublesome in-laws, who was pregnant and who didn't want to be. I had heard my mother talk with the other women about those things. Why wouldn't the whales be concerned as well? I watched the young ones swimming beside their mothers, happy for the salt toys of the sea.

I wished I had a sister. Even a brother would have been all right with me. Some days the puffins and the icebergs didn't seem to be enough. I pretended that the floating masses of ice were boats and that I could sail away on them to other coves. The gulls would cheer me on my journey. There were more birds here than I had learned to count, and that's a lot.

I went to the school in the village. That year I'd sat with the second graders. I thought that I knew a lot about lots of things. Gram told me that I had smarts. She looked after me most of the time. She said that my mother was in a battle with a spirit. For weeks she would stay in her bed; then one morning, I would come into the kitchen expecting the tea to be cold and there was Ma, cooking up a storm and talking to the walls at the same time. She was having a one-way conversation with someone, waving her stirring spoon, dripping oats and

Chapter 2 - The Boy on the Rock

milk and making no sense at all. I didn't know what was wrong, but Gram said that Ma would get better, we needed to have hope and prayers, and it would come about. She didn't say how long that might take.

On the days when Ma got frantic about things, it seemed I couldn't do anything fast enough. She turned into a master that could not be appeased. Do this, get that, fill the kettle, salt the fish, pick the carrots, collect the eggs. And then, like a gramophone winding down, she was back in her bed, unable to do so much as fix herself a cuppa tea. Gram looked after me and Da when Ma was in her bed. Da went out with the boats before the sun woke up. He and his brothers worked long days to bring in enough fish to sell so we could have what to live on. When Gram was in charge of things, I had time to visit with Nathaniel. He was my only friend outside of school. The bus came a long way from the other side of the village to pick me up, and there were no other children nearby.

Irish Mist

I remember the first time I saw him, the little boy on the rock. The clouds hung low and grey, and the wind was wild enough to steal my hat. Ma was in one of her crazy busy moods and was vexed with me. It seemed that once again I had done something not to her liking. As I heard her call out my first name, I stopped what I was doing. By the time she had started on my third name I was disappearing around the side of the house and heading for the cove. I liked to look for sea glass and odd-shaped stones. I was busy picking out amber pieces when I looked up at a gull flying past. Nathaniel was quietly sitting on the flat-topped rock, watching me. We introduced ourselves to each other in a most polite and proper way. Then I giggled, and he laughed too. We were quite proud of how we had known to do that, saying how do you do and such. But it was funny, the two of us, six and eight years of age we were, and acting like adults.

There was room on the rock for the two of us to sit beside each other. We sat like an old couple and looked at the sea. We talked about plain things: flowers and whales and bird poop. He said that he could understand the whale's song. Nathaniel told me, in his matter-of-fact little boy way, that he was six years old. He said it was hard to explain where he was from; he would save that bit until we knew each other better.

He must have been poor because he always wore the same set of overalls and the same green shirt. He had a thick flannel jacket with a missing button, and he wore tall rubber boots. They looked more than a size too big for him. Maybe he wore two pairs of socks.

Chapter 2 - The Boy on the Rock

Some of the kids at school would put newspaper in the toes of their boots to fill up the extra space until their feet grew longer, but that did nothing to keep you warm. I hoped he had double socks. His cap was a bit large for his head as well, but he didn't seem to mind. He said he would grow into it. He never did do that. When it started to rain, we said goodbye and "hope to see you again."

I ran back to the house as fast as I could. Storms on this side of The Rock came up fast, and the strong winds could carry me off the cliff if I didn't hurry. I was soaked to the skin by the time I got in the door. Thankfully, Ma was busy chatting with the walls and didn't notice.

There must have been a whole week of rain. I thought that flowers needed sunshine to grow. Not so in Newfoundland. Gram said it was like that in Ireland too. The shoots came up from the ground regardless. Well, she was right because I could see the leaves coming on the berry bushes and the daffodils were showing their yellow bud tops. When the sun finally broke through, the world shimmered with new life. I thought there were fairies who came and drank up the glistening pearls of rain drops that nature left behind especially for them. The deep green hillsides were rich with fresh growth, and the sky of clouds parted in greeting. Jack pines and mountain alder, black spruce and balsam fir waved to me as the calmed breeze moved through their branches.

Irish Mist

It was going to be a sunny day. I managed to disappear before anyone could notice that the eggs were still waiting in the coop. I wanted to see if Nathaniel was at the cove again. Perhaps we could play a game.

It was strange. At first he wasn't there and then he was. I had looked down, being careful about where I put my feet on the rocks, and when I had looked back up he was sitting there, staring out to sea. I had been ready to ask him about that bit of strangeness, but he was so happy to see me and started talking right away. It would have been rude of me to interrupt. He pointed out the family of otters playing in the waves, sliding down the bank into the water and then climbing back up to do it again. We watched them for a while and then decided on a game of chase, just the two of us.

And so it went, all summer and into late August. As we sat eating handfuls of blueberries one afternoon, I asked him if he would be at the school in September. I knew he had been too young the year before, otherwise I would have seen him there. His answer surprised me: *it was difficult*, he had said. Difficult wasn't an answer that explained anything to an eight year old.

Never You Mind, Newfoundland

Our outport, called Never You Mind, was a small collection of rustic houses and outbuildings far away from the things of modern man. There were no offices or movie theaters, no fancy stores or car dealerships. This place was about the sea, the fish that lived in it

Chapter 2 - The Boy on the Rock

and the waves that guarded it, the birds that flew over it and the boats that sailed on it. We lived by the tides; time was of less importance. The community had a dock with a fish-drying station and up the hill from that was the ship's chandler. The large room upstairs of it served as a meeting hall for families and individuals, for whatever they wished to meet about. The church doubled as a school, and there was not much else. One of the women might provide hairdressing or tailoring services. Another might make moonshine. It was a simple existence. Family, friends, and neighbours were everything that was important. We grew what we could, and caught the rest.

At the end of the day, if all the men made it home safely, then it was a good day. Every birth was celebrated and every death was mourned. There was so much that we didn't know was missing from our lives. That is one thing of many that makes me thankful. Not knowing was so much better than wanting. We had food, we had warmth, the old roof kept us dry. The house badly needed a coat of paint, but we had clean clothes and a rope swing. My mother's illness was part of life, just like how Da was always smelling of fish. I didn't know any other way.

Gram lived in the small attic room under the roof. She had moved into the house with us many years ago after her husband and two sons had died in the war and before I was born. She had no other relatives in Newfoundland that she knew of, and there was nowhere else for her to go. Her daughter Margaret's two younger sisters had moved away several years ago.

Irish Mist

Margaret and now I, Maisie, were the only family she had, still living, on The Rock. Gram knew way too much about loss; she'd lost two children. And now it pained her greatly that despite all her knowledge of herbs and things she could not lift the curse of sadness from Margaret.

When I was born, there was much hope that all would be well again, and it was at first. Margaret had smiled; the new baby was the tonic that was needed to bring joy back into the house. But it didn't last long. Within the year her depression returned, and its gloom of sadness veiled her life again.

It was the middle of September before I found a way to spend some time by myself. I hadn't seen Ma in two days. She was in her bed again. Gram had spent most of August busy with canning. Beans and peas were put up in jars, while carrots, potatoes, onions, and turnips were stored in the root cellar. She had made jellies and relishes, there were jars of berries in syrup, and now she was on to tomatoes. There were more tomatoes that year than we had jars to put them in. Before Gram could find another thing for me to do, I was out the door and around the side of the house.

I only saw Nathaniel the one time after school started. He didn't get on the bus with the other kids. I thought maybe he lived in the next village and went to the *other* church school. Da would have a fit if he found out that I had a friend who was Protestant. It made no sense to me. He had married a Protestant, so what was that about? Perhaps that was why we didn't

Chapter 2 - The Boy on the Rock

go to either church—we were not welcome. I figured it was best if I didn't ask which church Nathaniel's family belonged to; it was all the same to me. And not knowing meant that I would be able to be truthful if anyone should ask. Gram didn't care about any of that. *People was people,* she had said. She would give no place in her thinking to such things; she had left that behind her in Ireland. This should be new learning for everyone as far as she was concerned.

I ran down the grassy slope to the path and picked my way through the loose rocks to the cove. Nathaniel was sitting where I hoped he would be. I smiled and waved my welcome as I got closer. I remember that day like it was yesterday. I looked at his little boy face, and I was suddenly filled with sadness. I have no idea why, but it was overwhelming. I shifted my eyes to the sea, to see what it was that held his attention. There was nothing there. That was odd by itself: there should have been boats. I looked back to the little boy who sat on the rocks. There was nothing there. That was even more strange. I called his name. I searched around the big boulders and looked down the mud path where the otters had made their slide. I called again. Nathaniel was gone. I sat by myself on the rock and waited until the tide changed. I had no idea what to make of it. As I walked back to the house, the feeling of sadness persisted. I thought I should ask my Gram. She knew all things worth knowing; surely she would know about Nathaniel.

Irish Mist

Gramma Brigid Byrne

Gram was stirring something on the stove when I came in the door looking windblown and forlorn. The kettle was just starting to whistle. My nose twitched as the strong smell of herbs filled my nostrils. Gram was cooking up medicine. Someone must be sick.

I didn't know much about illness, but I recognized the smell of Gramma B's remedies. People would come from two outports away to get their hands on them. They traded whatever they could offer in exchange for her wisdom and her cures. The recipes had been passed down by her ancestors from the time before history was written. She told me that was why she wore the silver Owl on the chain around her neck. It had been handed down to her as well. As I opened my mouth to ask her about the little boy on the rock, she hushed me. Ma had gotten much worse throughout the afternoon. This was something different than what kept her in bed the rest of the time. This was not about spirits. It was something of this world that she was suffering from now.

Gram had been teaching me about her medicines, and I had learned to find the right herbs when she asked me to fetch them for her. Gram said I was a good helper. She had a section of the vegetable garden kept just for her plants. In the fall she wrapped them in cheesecloth and hung them with clothes pegs from strings along the low beams of the kitchen. When they were completely dried, she pressed the leaves into powders with her heavy rolling pin and put them

Chapter 2 - The Boy on the Rock

in labelled glass jars. She had me carry them, with great care, down the ladder into the dark, damp cellar. There they then sat, lined up on a dusty shelf like soldiers, waiting to be called into active duty.

The year was 1957. The influenza epidemic took many in that round, not as many as had died in 1951, but it left me an orphan. My mother was gone by the next morning, and my father and two of his brothers followed a week later. My father's family was unable to help us with much. They already had more mouths to feed than they could manage. Gram held back about talk of religious preferences. She did not want me to know that people would turn their backs if you thought differently about those things. So Gram became my Ma and my Da, which suited me fine. We didn't really see them anyway, the Calders; they seemed to think that there was something wrong with us even before my parents died. The brothers went out on the boats together, but that is where it stopped.

Uncle Cecil was different. He helped us as best he could. He brought us food when he had extra, he came along with a bucket of tar when the roof was leaking, he picked up the mail, and drove us into St. John's when we had need to go. Gram did her best to repay his kindness with the herbs that kept him and his family healthy through the cold, damp winter. The only other people that came to see Gramma B believed in the old religion. She burned sage and let the smoke from the tightly rolled leaves flow through every room in the house. The influenza defied even her medicine in many cases, but somehow, neither one of us got sick.

Irish Mist

We managed to get through the winter, the two of us, with what we had stored and what people brought to trade for Gramma B's medicines.

As the winter passed, so did its sadness. It still managed to creep in like the snow under the door, but for the most part Gram and I were busy with life, and we tried not to think about sad things. Lots of people seeking medicine made the trek to our oak-timbered door, and Gram was called on to birth a few babies as well.

We settled into a routine, and the days of rain and snow and howling winds were filled with what needed to be done. The simple task of washing clothes and sheets took an entire day, longer if the weather wasn't good. Sometimes it would be days before the damp went out of the bedding. We always had the fire going and that was a big help, but the smell of wet wool was always there. In the evenings there was sit-down stuff to do, mending and book reading. The large transistor radio that sat on the table with its hand-tatted doily in the front room was a great source of entertainment. Gram taught me to dance in our small, rustic kitchen. We turned up the sound and pushed the table against the wall. I was tall, and she wasn't, so it worked out nicely. We listened to all sorts of music. Gram said I needed a complete education. She taught me to play card games, counting games like cribbage and gin rummy. Living with Gram was more of an education than school ever was.

Chapter 2 - The Boy on the Rock

I remember the night that we finally talked about the little boy on the rock. Gram was working on the pile of mending that was always accumulating, and I was practicing my darning skills. She was patching my favourite overalls when I said that my friend wore patches on his pants and could I please have fancy-coloured ones like he did. She asked who that friend might be, as I had not mentioned him before.

"His name is Nathaniel," I started, "and he is six years old. I don't know where he lives or who his parents are. When I go to the cove he is there, sitting on the large rock at the bottom of the hill. He sits and stares out to the sea until he notices me coming, and then he smiles and waves."

Gram looked at me with wide eyes. "Go on," she said. "Tell me all about him." I thought she was just curious, but the more I said the more interested she got, to the point that her needlework lay in her lap, forgotten. "When did you see him last?"

I had to think for a moment; then it came to me in a rush. "Last fall, the day Ma was so sick and you were making medicine for her."

Gram gave a huge sigh and turned in her chair so she could face me directly. She began her tale. "It was the year before you were born. You did have a brother." She held up her hand to stop me: I would need to wait to ask my questions. "Your father named him Nathaniel after his own father. Such a good little boy, always minded his manners and did as he was told. He liked

Irish Mist

to sit by the cove and wait for the boats to come in. He was always watching those boats. He didn't care if it was raining or fog or both. He wanted to be a fisherman just like his Da. Of course he did. Well, it had rained for days and the rockslide came down so fast that no one would have been able to escape. He was swept away; there was nothing we could do. His wee body was never found. He was all of six years old."

"But Gram, I have seen him. He sits on the rock and watches the sea. Why is he there? Is he still waiting for the boats?"

Gram looked at me with love in her eyes. "You, my precious child, can see what most cannot." She touched the Owl charm that hung from the tarnished silver chain around her neck. "You have this too, the sight of things unseen." I was now completely confused. *My mother had talked to walls, my grandmother listened to owls, and I saw a little boy who wasn't there!*

Another Year Begins

Spring began to show its face. There were bits of shoots coming up in Gram's herb garden, and I could see tiny leaves on the stubby branches of the currant bushes. The rain had stopped for now, and Gram said that I could go and see if my friend would be wanting to play. She must have known that Nathaniel would be sitting on the rock waiting for me. I had wondered if I would see him again, but Gram always seemed to know.

Chapter 2 - The Boy on the Rock

I skipped down the slope, being careful of the muddy patches and flipping my chestnut braids around my head. As I picked my way through the rocky bits, I thought about something Gram had been talking about. She had said that maybe we had to give a good amount of thinking to moving to another place. There was no way on earth that we could manage another winter with just the two of us. She said she was getting too old to do the heavy stuff. I didn't think she was old. I thought she was perfect just the way she was. Well, there was one thing that I did notice. She usually did the mending in the evenings but found that the light was no longer good enough for threading the needle. I had no problem doing it for her but she said that was not the point and thank you very much. She had been busy writing letters instead, sealing them in fancy airmail envelopes, and addressing them to other places in Canada and to Ireland. I wondered what was in the letters she wrote. I would be nine by the end of the month, and I figured I was old enough to know what it was all about. There was no point in asking questions. She would tell me when it was time for me to know.

I saw him as I rounded the corner at the end of the path, same as always, sitting on the flat-topped rock and staring out to sea. He was still wearing the same shirt and overalls. As soon as he saw me, he started waving his little arm in the air to welcome me. He stood, and we gave each other a hug. He seemed shorter–or was it that I had gotten taller? It didn't matter to our friendship, and we resumed our conversation as if there had never been a winter between us.

Irish Mist

Nathaniel Graeme Calder

Nathaniel Graeme Calder was born in the fall of 1942. He was the firstborn child of Margaret and Graeme Calder and a second generation Canadian of Celtic roots. He was a fine lad and had a shock of flame-red hair from birth. His parents thought he was perfect. As he grew into a wee man, he talked of becoming a fisherman like his Da and his uncles. He lived on an island in the middle of the Atlantic ocean, or it might as well be in the middle—there was nothing to see for miles and miles. Nothing but the sea. What else could he want to be?

By the time he was five, he could name almost all of the many species of whales that came by the cove where he lived. He could look in the nets as they were hauled ashore and name each type of fish as they were loaded onto the dock. He knew that the gulls carried secrets to the fish and the puffins watched it all happen. He was sure of it. He loved to watch the icebergs as they floated along and wondered if, someday, he might travel on them to where they came from or went to. His little face was covered in freckles and his toothy grin was always a delight to see.

Each day, when the slack tide would bring the men in to shore with the boats, he would sit at the bottom of the hill and wait for his Da. When it was raining, little Nathaniel wore a Macintosh over his clothes, with a matching wide-brimmed hat. He always wore his gum boots. Rain or shine. The two of them would walk back to the house together, and the father would

Chapter 2 - The Boy on the Rock

share stories of his day with his treasured son. They were quite the pair those two, that is what Gram said. Margaret would watch from the house as they made their way up the grassy slope, chatting about fish and whales and nets and boats. Sometimes Graeme would lift his son up on his shoulders and carry him along. When they got to the door, they both smelled like fish.

Margaret was just beginning to grow the new little one in her belly. She didn't even know that Maisie was there. On the day that poor wee Nathaniel Graeme Calder died, the world stopped spinning on its axis, just for a few moments in time. His parents, family, and friends mourned the passing of his young life with the sad understanding that this was the reality of life. Margaret was beside herself with grief and could be heard singing his favourite songs, as though she believed he could still hear his mother's voice. Graeme did as men often did: he went back to earning a living for his family. He knew no other way.

Gramma Byrne knew that Nathaniel would always be sitting on the flat-topped rock, wearing his gum boots and colourfully-patched overalls. He was there still, and would always be, waiting. He waited for the boats to come in, he waited for his Da, and he waited for the tides to change. Then one day, he began waiting for Maisie, his sister, to come and find him so that they could play. He hoped to tell her the words to the songs the whales sang. He wanted to share the secrets that the gulls whispered to the fish. And one day, on a warm and sunny afternoon, with the breeze being just right, they would sail to distant coves on a fancy iceberg, with dolphins and leatherback sea turtles as their escorts, puffins waving to them from the shore. In Newfoundland, that just might be what brothers and sisters did. He was waiting to find out.

And It Came To Pass

The three letters addressed to Gram had sat waiting to be picked up at the post office for almost a week. Uncle Cecil had brought them to the house for her when he came looking for some cough medicine. They were all in fancy airmail envelopes, just like the ones Gram had used to send her own letters. One was from Ireland, and the other two were from Canada. Gram put the kettle on to boil and finished up the breakfast dishes. Only when the tea had been poured into our cups did she open the first letter. It was from her brother, who still lived in Ireland. It was short and to the point. In his opinion, returning to Ireland was not a good idea. It was still a difficult place for women. If Brigid wished to return to the homeland, she would need to marry. Would she like for him to arrange for a suitor?

The second letter was from her aunt who lived on the west coast of Canada. She said that she had taken a fall. Her daughter, Denise, was looking after her for now. She was unsure if she would have to move in with them temporarily. She offered apologies, there was nothing she could do to help.

The third letter came from Saskatchewan. My Aunt Sybil, one of my mother's younger sisters, had a large

Chapter 2 - The Boy on the Rock

room that was currently unused. She said that she would love for us to come and stay. She could always use the help. Her husband Ray had no problem with our doing that, Sybil continued to say. He was probably too busy to even notice. All that was required was that we earn our keep. There was a small school in the local church, and there were other children for me to play with. It would be wonderful to have a child in the house, as she and Ray had been unable to have any themselves.

Gram looked up from the letter in her hands. "Well child, my guess is that our options are few. We need to be making our plans. It will do us no good to stay here. We do not have enough money to sustain us. I have no interest in a suitor. Your other aunt did not bother or could not reply. In my mind this must be our choice." She touched the Owl charm that hung on its tarnished silver chain around her neck. What do you think?"

What did I think? I thought the adventure might be what I wished for. Did they have icebergs in Saskatchewan?

Irish Mist

Chapter 3
The Trees that Grow Old

This is a happy story, the sad bits will not be found here. It is a tale of finding joy in the act of taking a walk in the woods.

Irish Mist

The western red cedars grow tall, and the Douglas firs grow even taller. Many of the trees on Vancouver Island are centuries old and measure up to nine metres in circumference. Within the heart of each of these ancient conifers lives a spirit. This is a story about seven of them, only a few of the many who live here. They play among the maples and the hemlock, float in the streams, and sit in the mist atop the waterfalls. The lodgepole pines provide homes for the bald eagles, and the cedar waxwings sing wherever they go. It is the perfect playground for the little ones who need a place to be while they wait for their guardians to arrive and offer them a new home.

This is a well-organized forest, despite its haphazard look. Mother Nature knows the delicate balance that needs to be nurtured so that everyone and everything can succeed. Walking along the rustic paths that weave throughout the park is a walk into the mystic. The smells of earth and water are intense. The air is filled with birdsong, carried on the currents of ancient trees that caress the skin and soothe the soul. Fallen leaves and pine needles form a soft carpet; it's like walking in a pair of comfy slippers. Between rotting stumps, decomposing branches, and mounds of fern-covered soil there are large pools of water, a looking glass to the sky.

The trees in Cathedral Grove live in a variety of circumstances; standing upright and strong, some with hollowed-out middles, large enough to envelop a person. Others have fallen and are left to decay in their own time. The uprooted ones display their undersides, bleached like bones and as intricately woven as macramé rib cages.

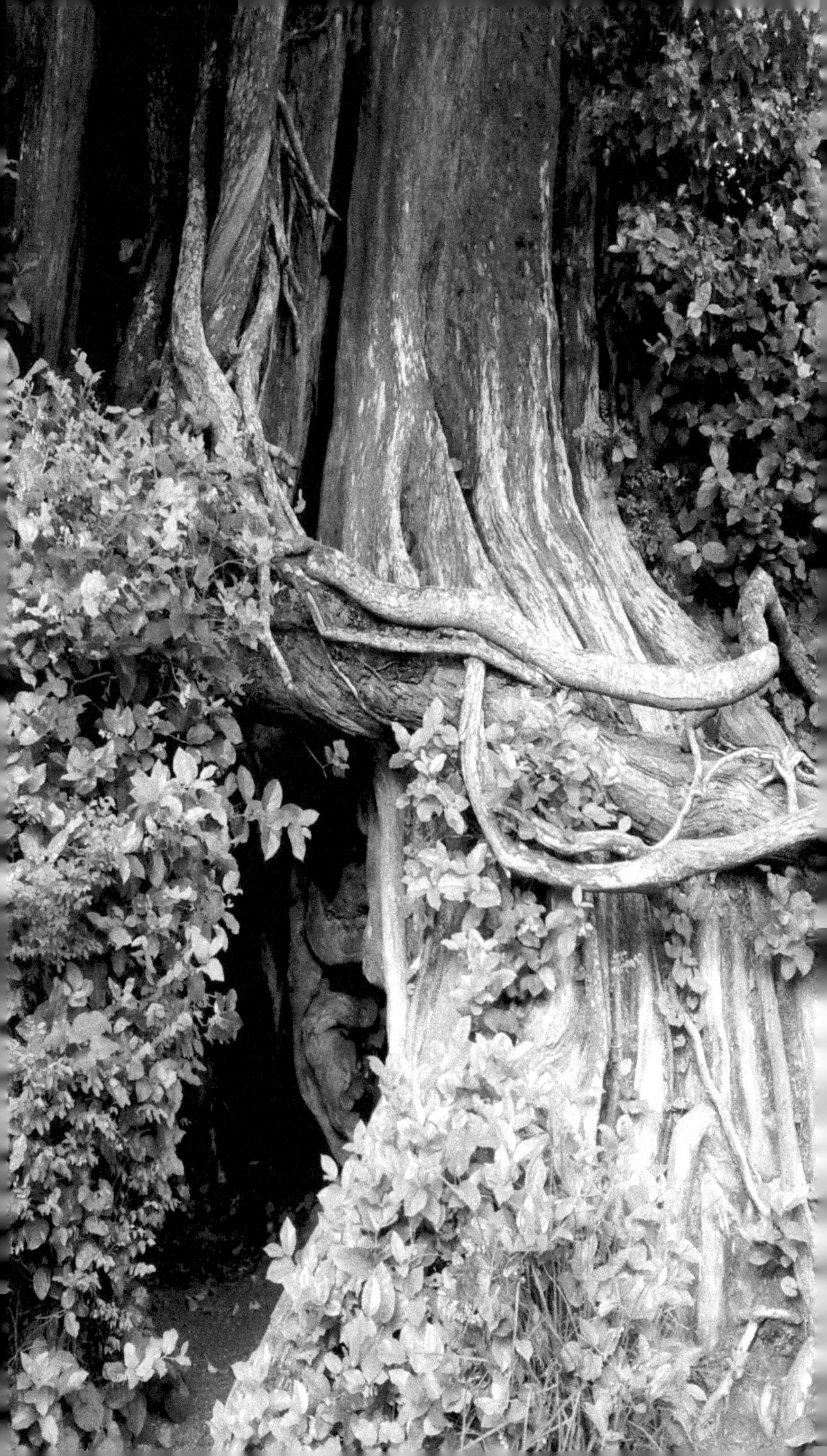

Irish Mist

There is a spirit in every one of them. Children do not die of old age and sadly, many of the child spirits are too wounded by their untimely passing to help others yet. They will be given the time that they need to absorb the healing that comes from the treetops and waterfalls, the birdsong and the morning dew. The ones who have been made whole again are sorted into groups. When the guardians have offered themselves to the children, the next group moves forward. Very well organized, indeed.

This particular covey of spirits is made up of seven little people. The original expectation was that they would have grown old in the world, the reality is that they now live in old trees, no longer of the world. I have put them in alphabetical order, which might be helpful if you are trying to remember who is who; Abner, Bonita, Clara, Daniel, Eric, Francis and Georgiane. Regardless of how they came to be here, it has become their waiting place. Nothingness is not an option to be considered, regardless of whether it exists or not.

The #19 Highway that comes up from Nanaimo along the east coast of the island divides itself just before Coombs. One section continues on to Port Hardy at its northern tip. Turning inland, it becomes the #4, winding its way along the shore of Cameron Lake, through MacMillan Provincial Park and westward to the Pacific ocean. Cathedral Grove lies within the park's boundaries. From there the road leads to Port Alberni, where it becomes the Pacific Rim Highway. It then continues to weave its way to the west coast of the island and Ucluelet. If the traveller takes the time to stop on the shore and look across the Pacific Ocean,

Chapter 3 - The Trees that Grow Old

they can envision Japan. Turning northward along the road will bring you into Tofino, a storm watcher's delight and a town filled with eclectic, artsy people. The road from here to there is a pleasant drive with good pavement and spectacular scenery. It is travelled by many people each day, for a variety of reasons.

On this day, there are hundreds of travellers on this road. Many of them will stop and walk through the grove of huge trees. Among the ones who stop, there are seven people who will choose to do more. They will listen. The reason for their stop is inconsequential, the fact that they will listen to the child spirits that live here is the point. And they don't even know it yet! The children of the trees have much to offer, but only those who are willing to believe in things unseen will understand their gift.

The Cast & Crew: The Child Spirits

Abner is just a little guy, still very much a young child, full of curiosity. Despite that, he is shy and seems to be forever in need of reassurances. He's a bit on the chubby side, which only adds to his charm. His beautiful brown eyes can look into a person's soul and see the insecurities that lie there. He understands what it is that stops people from moving forward.

Bonita, pretty as her name suggests, has an attitude that says she is her own boss. She is adamant that no one should mess with that. Her take-charge way of dealing with life's challenges is inspiring, and her boldness is infectious. She encourages people to speak their truth, regardless of what others might think. She believes that life is worth living, and the best way to do that is to get out there and do it.

Clara is graceful and slender of build. She is famous in this neck of the woods for her ability to dance through the trees without tripping over roots or stumbling over rocks. Her logical mind can find a path through the obstacles of greed and negativity. She is the one who is able to guide the lost through the maze of life, showing the way to the things that are real.

Daniel often wears a frown upon his face. He is a serious-minded soul and wants to know the details of everything before he acts. He is always thinking, sometimes to the point that he becomes oblivious to what is around him. If you have a problem that needs to be solved, he will not stop until he has found a solution that matches your need to know. He is the epitome of perseverance.

Eric loves to explore. He is a light-hearted lad with blond hair and bright blue eyes. He is forever off searching for a new species of insect or bird at the far reaches of the grove and beyond and therefore is most often late for everything. Eric is all about epiphanies and finding little gems in unexpected places. He is the silver lining.

Francis' empathy knows no boundaries. He will listen to every woe and lament without judgement. He is a bit of a Friar Tuck, warm and supportive, jovial

Chapter 3 - The Trees that Grow Old

and quick with helpful suggestions. His ability to read between the lines of a person's life-book is exceptional. He is always at the ready with his kind demeanour to enlighten the thoughts of others.

Georgiane, the eldest of the group, is pure joy to know. She likes to dance and sing and hug with no reserves. Her boundless energy and enthusiasm can move mountains. And she does, all the time. One of her heart-and-soul hugs can be the gift of a changed life to a person in need. She is joy in its purest form.

These are the child spirits, waiting for their new homes. They are eager to make a difference in the lives of seven special travellers, on a sunny day, in a grove of trees.

The Cast & Crew: The Travellers

Alan is on his way to Port Alberni. He is a salesman for a pharmaceutical firm and has a series of appointments with local doctors on the island. When he is finished today, he will drop the rental car at the airport and get on a plane for his flight to Montreal. He's a long way from home. He is trying his best to follow all the guidelines that guarantee success at the art of salesmanship. Unfortunately, that also means he is constantly on the road.

He is so stressed that he can barely be the loving, thoughtful husband that he truly wants to be. He loves children and can hardly wait to be a father of a big family. The image of a long harvest table, covered

Irish Mist

with large serving bowls of food and surrounded by children busy with feeding themselves, arms reaching across each other for more potatoes or the ketchup bottle, is his vision for himself and Jocelyne.

He desperately needs to succeed, but that scares him too. What if he really doesn't want to be a salesman? What if he gets good at it and then he's trapped in a job that offers only money as a reward? He comes up to the sign for the Provincial Park. It displays a restroom icon. He had better stop here.

Ben is on his last run of the week. Every day he drives from the pick-up point at the ferry terminal in Nanaimo to the west coast of the island and back again. Every day, three hours across and three hours back, load and unload, a full day's work. Ben has been driving a courier truck for longer than he should. Many years ago he had lost interest in the scenery, the bald eagles and the hawks, the beautiful blue of the lakes, and the flow of the streams along his route. He was bored. Bored with his job and bored with his crummy apartment in a building with a broken elevator. All he ever did on his time off was sit and watch TV or play video games. He was even tired of his friends. They knew nothing of what really kept him a private man. When he did go out, it was to the local watering hole where he sat with the same sorry group of losers and talked about nothing.

He takes a swig from his thermos and starts thinking about the ham sandwich loaded with tomatoes and lettuce and garlic mayonnaise in his lunch box

Chapter 3 - The Trees that Grow Old

that he will enjoy while the crew unloads his cargo. The sign for the park is coming up soon and he's ahead of schedule. He could stop and stretch his legs, maybe take a bite of his sandwich.

Connor is in his mid-forties, divorced, and looking for some action. He drives a sporty little number, metallic black with a tan leather interior. Of course, it is a convertible. It boasts a high-end sound system to match his high-end attitude, a far cry from the way he actually feels about himself. When he looks in the mirror in the mornings nowadays, a middle-aged man stares back at him, one who has needed to modify the way he combs his hair.

This is not Connor's idea of living the dream, but it is the best he can come up with. He was supposed to do great things: there was supposed to be more for him in this life. He feared his Irish heritage was letting him down. Where was his vitality? His ready-for-anything, "real man" persona, had deserted him. What had happened to the claps on his back that had encouraged him to live as if the world was his oyster? It was looking more like a sardine now. Small, undesirable, and only good for feeding the bigger fish. Connor, the dreamer, is on his way to Tofino. There is a sweet-looking cuddy cabin cruiser for sale in the marina. *He could call it his canoodling cabin!* As he navigates the bend of the #4 that passes through The Grove, he notices some good-looking ladies walking across the parking lot. He quickly downshifts and pulls in the exit before he loses sight of their short-short covered backsides.

Irish Mist

Denise is on her way to visit her mother in Ucluelet. She is fraught with worry over the zillion things going wrong in her life. Her mother is aging and in ill health. Soon Denise and her mother will need to have "the talk" about selling her house and moving into a retirement home. Her husband seems to be growing tired of their relationship. He has been aloof towards her, vague about lateness at work, and when he does come home, he buries his face in the newspaper. Her teenage daughter has a new boyfriend that scares the hell out of her. He even looks scary. He has a motorcycle and motorcycle friends. Denise has no idea how to fix any of it, and the swirling of fears in her head has left her so muddled that she can no longer think.

So she shops. She shops a lot. It keeps her too busy to spend time thinking about anything besides shopping. She buys more and more stuff with the hope that at some point, hopefully before she runs out of money, she will be able to face the mess of her life. She sees the sign that advertises walking trails and decides that clearing out some of the cobwebs that muddle her brain before she arrives at her mother's house would be a smart thing to do.

Esther is pregnant. She has known this for quite a while and yet, she still has not decided what she should do, or even what she wants to do. The father, a goodlooking surfer boy from Tofino, does not know about this new life growing in her belly. There really is no point in telling him. Esther sees this as her situation and not his. Right or wrong, this is how she feels. She still has hopes for her life, starting with

Chapter 3 - The Trees that Grow Old

finding her way through this. She has skills; she speaks three languages: English, French (courtesy of her French Canadian father), and the native tongue of her mother's people, the Mi'kmaq. She has worked as a tourist guide in an office and in the wilderness, and she has a particularly good talent for sizing people up, despite the fact that she had been fooled by a handsome face. In her mind she can hear her grandmother's voice telling her that this child is a gift, just as she had been.

Esther knows that this great responsibility is hers, even before her baby's face sees the sun. She has come to the Grove for guidance from the earth and the trees, the only one of the travellers looking for an epiphany.

Frances, or Frannie as she prefers, loves her Honda Civic. It is an older model, with the tell-tale rust eating away at the wheel wells and its bumper held secure by a repurposed wire coat hanger. The once deep blue paint looks like someone has spilt milk on it and never bothered to clean it up. Frannie is a woman of large proportions and fills the driver's seat to capacity. The rest of the car is filled as well, almost to the roof in places. She has an apartment in Coombs and travels every week to visit her therapist in Port Alberni.

Frannie is a hoarder. There! She said it out loud, if only to herself. Her landlord has threatened to evict her if she does not get her obsessive behaviour under control. It started when she was a teen, after the house fire that claimed the life of her cat. She couldn't even think of having another pet, but she did love to watch the dog walkers in the Grove. She drives into the park entrance, ready to enjoy the sight of people leading normal lives.

Greg is excited about the tourist season. It is always the most lucrative time of the year for him, and Vancouver Island is a magnet for tourists. The mild climate, along with its varied landscapes offers scenery, flora and fauna, sport and adventure, relaxation, shopping and dining. Whatever the focus of a visitor to the Island, they all have two things in common: money in their wallets and a keen interest in pursuing the purpose for their visit. They are prime targets for a quick-fingered thief with a bit of intuition and creativity. Greg has not always been a thief. There was a time that he was just a little boy. Trusting and hopeful. Well, life isn't like that, now is it? Shit happens and a person has to do what he can to survive. The sad bit is that you just keep on doing it. It is the only way you know.

Just off to the side of the Alberni Highway is the big parking lot belonging to MacMillan Provincial Park. It is looking pretty full today. He thinks he might stop in and see if he can make himself some extra gas money.

These are the people whose lives will be changed because they are willing to be changed, on a sunny day, in a grove of trees.

Chapter 3 - The Trees that Grow Old

Alan & Abner

Alan parked as close to the comfort station as he could manage: the lot was full of tourists. It was a bit of a walk but it was a pleasant day, and he didn't mind the break. He used the restroom and stepped back outside. Something caught his eye and he found his feet being pulled in that direction. Despite all the rules governing the success of a salesman, he couldn't resist the heavenly draw of the woodsy smells. Now he wasn't even sure what had caught his eye.

Abner tugged at his pant leg. "Hello," he said. "How are you today? My name is Abner. Will you help me find my way home?"

"Well, young man, I would be happy to help. Where do you think your parents might be? Is that who we should be looking for, or are you here with a school group?"

Alan is a kind man, despite the driving, competitive nature required of a salesman. Perhaps that is why he hates his job. That by itself is a worry. He had been with the company for barely six months. He did not want to become the personality type that the job required him to be. He looked at the boy, with his beautiful brown eyes and curly hair. Alan waited for him to answer. When Abner started to cry instead, he swivelled his head, looking in all directions for an adult searching for a child. When he turned back to the child, Abner had disappeared. He had found his way home. Alan looked around him again, but the

Irish Mist

little boy had definitely gone. *Or so he thought.* Alan left the path, returned to his car, and got back on the road for Port Alberni.

As he drove, he found himself sorting out a few things in his mind. He thought about why he had even become a salesman in the first place. He never thought he would be successful at school. College was not something he wanted to spend money on. There was the trade school, but he had been unable to narrow his focus to one skill. He was more of a jack-of-all-trades kind of guy. His mind wandered with the curves in the road and in an instant a clear thought came to him. He had been convinced of his failure and now he was afraid of success. How twisted was that? He parked the car in the lot beside the medical office, took his heavy sample case from the trunk and went into the building.

Alan had finished his appointments for the week. He drove his rental car to the small airport and tossed his keys in the drop-off box. He went through the motions of clearing the security measures and picked out a seat for himself by the window of the building. He did not have long to wait, and in short order he was on his way to the mainland where he would catch his connecting flight to Montreal. Jocelyne would meet him at the airport, which was not far from their home. He could hardly wait.

The flight layover in Vancouver was two hours long, so he went to one of the many takeout counters

Chapter 3 - The Trees that Grow Old

to get himself a coffee and a sandwich. He was having a hard time finding a place to sit as it was late afternoon and the bars were full of businessmen waiting to fly east. He carried his overnight bag in one hand and balanced the tray holding his turkey club sandwich and coffee with the other. Finally, he saw a table for two with a guy sitting alone, nursing a beer. Alan introduced himself and expressed his frustration at finding a place to sit. The man smiled and responded to Alan in good English, coloured by a thick French accent. Yes, he was most welcome to join him.

They exchanged small details about themselves. Alan felt comfortable with the conversation and confided to André that he was unhappy with his current employment. André was self-employed and worked mostly from home. He loved his job. He went on to explain what it was that he did for a living. Alan barely noticed when their flight was announced over the loudspeaker. The two men were able to negotiate a seat change so they could sit beside each other, and the conversation continued until they landed at the Dorval Airport almost five hours later.

It was late in the evening—the cross-country time change was always a challenge—and the men were tired after the long flight. They exchanged business cards and committed to carrying on their relationship. Alan greeted his wife, Jocelyne, with a sweep-you-off-your-feet hug. He twirled her around in the air like a new bride. He could not wait to talk with her about his new ideas. Jocelyne had some excitement of her own to share.

Irish Mist

It was a situation of you-go-first/no-you-go-first until their laughter stopped the process. Jocelyne placed her hand on her belly. There was no mistaking her gesture. Alan was beside himself with joy. They were going to have a child! He twirled her in the air again, a bit more gently this time. He asked all the father-to-be questions he could think of as Jocelyne smiled her biggest, brightest smile. "Alan, what is it that you want to tell me?"

The young couple settled on the huge Sally Ann sale couch that half-filled the living room of their duplex flat. Alan took Jocelyne's hands in his and told her the story of meeting André in Vancouver airport. "He and his wife are foster parents. They have a big house, and it's full of children in need of care. He says it is hard work: the children have been damaged by their situations and there is conflict. Just keeping up with the housekeeping is a challenge. But they love it and the rewards are huge. These kids will have a second chance to become the best they can be. It pays well too. They have enough for their own needs, and he works from home." He paused and looked inquiringly at his best friend: his wife and now the mother of his child. "What do you think, chérie? Can we do this?" He quickly added, "I would need to go back to school. There are courses I'd have to take to become an administrator. There are educational grants to cover the costs, and we could ask your parents for a loan."

Jocelyne thought about it for perhaps five seconds. She was thrilled. She saw the layers of insecurity fall away from her husband like an onion, revealing his sweet soul.

Chapter 3 - The Trees that Grow Old

Ben & Bonita

Ben found a spot to park at the far end of the lot. Courier trucks take up a bit more space than a car, and he didn't want to be denting any doors. People got cranky about things like that, and he didn't want complaints complicating his uncomplicated life. All he wanted was to eat some of his sandwich and take a few swigs from his enormous thermos of coffee. He had added something extra to the brew, just to keep things mellow on the road. As he sat in the shade, he noticed how beautiful the tree beside him was. It had been years since he had even looked at the shape of a tree. He screwed the lid back on his thermos, re-wrapped the sandwich, locked the door of his cab, and stepped down to the pavement. He raised his arms to the sky and stretched. *The sky sure is blue today!*

He started walking towards the hiking trail, thinking that he had fifteen minutes to spare. Bonita was standing and looking at the trail map, a confused look on her face. "Excuse me," she said. "I can't figure out these damn maps! Can you help me?"

This is turning into a very interesting day. When was the last time a pretty girl asked me for anything? Ben straightened his back and sucked in his gut despite the fact that girls were not his interest. Any interest in his person was worth sucking in his gut. "I think I can make sense of it for you. Where do you want to go?"

"Well," she answered, "I was hoping to do the trail loop. My boyfriend said it was too far, but I am not

Irish Mist

letting him tell me what I can and cannot do. He is all worried that I will get lost or tired or fall into a pit. I figure that if I fall in a pit, some strong and handsome stranger will pull me out. If I get tired, I can sit down. *Lost* could go either way, but here you are to help with that. All good, right?"

Ben marvelled at her sense of perspective. He needed a little more of that in his life. He pointed out the *You Are Here* arrow and explained the marker posts and distances to her. She smiled and thanked him, picked up her backpack and went off to find her chosen trail. Ben walked around for another bit, enjoying the sounds of the birds and the fresh air.

He got back in the truck and continued on to his next drop-off point. He reached across the seat for his thermos as he drove. *Maybe I shouldn't be doing that, said the voice in his head.* He pulled his hand back and adjusted the radio instead.

Ben arrived at his last pick-up point of the day. He had dumped out the rest of his cold coffee, and he was hungry. The ham sandwich that he had consumed earlier in the day was nothing but a memory. He still had more than three hours on the road before he got home. He stopped for a coffee and a Danish at the yummy German bakery in Ucluelet before he made the rest of the drive.

He had his brown-bagged cheese Danish in his hand, a fresh coffee in his thermos, and was on his

Chapter 3 - The Trees that Grow Old

way to his truck when he noticed a man standing with his thumb out on the side of the road. Ben was feeling generous. He knew he wasn't supposed to pick up riders, but then, he wasn't supposed to be drinking on the job either.

The guy looked clean and sober. *Why not give him a ride?* He would enjoy some company and conversation. *Where the heck did that thought come from?* Brian, the hitchhiker, was more than happy for the lift. He was going to Qualicum and hopefully he would be able to stay with a friend for a bit, but he didn't know that for sure yet. He had made some bad decisions for himself and, well, he had no place to go. Over the course of the next two hours Brian shared his story of dead ends and poor judgement. Ben could well understand the bad decisions that people made when it came to life. He had done nothing with his. Perhaps his attitude of waiting for life to happen wasn't working so well for him. Maybe it was time for him to be the boss of his own life and make things happen for himself. He looked at the man beside him. He offered Brian his couch for the weekend. This could be a new beginning for both of them.

Ben's small apartment was a huge surprise to Brian. Ben never shared his private space with anyone. It was too personal. This was a huge step out for the trucker. Ben shifted his weight from foot to foot as he waited with apprehension for Brian's reaction. He was second guessing himself about his decision to bring someone he had only just met into his home, a home that said everything about himself. His gut told him that Brian was a good man. He needed to follow through with that and believe that living his truth was a far better thing than living a lie.

The first thing that Brian noticed when he walked in was the orderly look of the place, followed by the fresh scent of laundry recently done. He looked around the corner to see a well-organized kitchen with utensils and shiny pots displayed on hooks. Everything was neat and tidy and clean. Brian put his duffel down in the entrance way and removed his hiking boots. He could not believe what was right in front of him. He turned to his new friend and his eyes filled with tears. What a wonderful day, hopefully just the beginning of many wonderful days ahead.

Ben put his keys on the table by the door. He was home, and that was a good thing. He had no idea where his new sense of self had come from, but the energy flow of freedom made him smile.

Connor & Clara

Connor loves the sound of the revving engine and the throaty exhaust when he downshifts. His sweet little ride makes him feel good about himself. He had paid some big bucks for that, meaning the car. He didn't see his acquisitions as buying self-esteem, that was just a bonus—or was it? He scanned the parking lot: the two ladies in the short-shorts, the reason for his quick detour from the road, were just going into the comfort station. He got out of the car, adjusted his pants, and finger-combed his hair. Connor leaned

Chapter 3 - The Trees that Grow Old

against the driver's door, tossing his keys in the air while he thought up a few good pick-up lines and tried to look casual. He felt the car move as he heard the clunk.

"Oh shit!" a voice blurted out from the other side of his car. He turned around to see a woman standing with her hand covering her mouth, a look of horror on her face. "Oh my gosh! I am so sorry! The wind caught my door. Oh my gosh! I can't believe that it did that. Damn! There's a dent in your door. Oh. Shit."

Connor almost vaulted himself across the hood of his car and around to the passenger side. There was indeed a large dent in his door. That is what happens when something very sturdy, such as the door of a pickup truck, forcefully collides with something constructed to look pretty. Yes. A large, ugly dent. The woman was talking now, giving him bits of information and introducing herself. "Well, isn't this an interesting way to meet people. My name is Clara," she said as she held out her hand.

Connor pulled his eyes from the dent to the woman who had done the damage. He was ready to give her a self-righteous blast about the cost of repairs and the major inconvenience to which he had now been put. He was gearing up a full head of steam when he looked at her and immediately shut his mouth.

Clara was everything he was not. Her flannel shirt and worn jeans, wispy, *au naturel* hair and unmanicured hands said everything about her person that he thought he needed to know. The rusty old pickup confirmed the profile. He was dealing with a country hick. What shut his mouth was not her outward appearance, but the sound of her voice and the words she spoke. He was completely baffled. The irony of the situation was not lost on him; his agenda had been to pick up a few ladies and he had been hit by a pickup. The big surprise in this was that he liked Clara—instantly.

He forgot about the ladies in the short-shorts and listened to Clara as she told him about her brother who owned a body shop. Before he could express his preference for wanting a professional service, she had him convinced to give her brother's place a try. Floyd's shop was located on the outskirts of Tofino, not far from the marina. Since he was headed that way, he decided that giving a local garage a look-see might be a good idea.

Connor followed the directions he had been given and arrived at Floyd's Body Shop after his appointment with the boat seller at the marina. The boat had been a shipwreck, not his idea of anything close to mint condition and certainly not a place where any hanky-panky might occur. When he got to Floyd's garage he was feeling more than a bit skeptical about the service that might be available. There were old cars everywhere, and none of them looked repaired. What he didn't see was the sleek, new custom paint jobs on the very expensive foreign cars parked behind the building. Clara was there as promised, clad in mechanic's

Chapter 3 - The Trees that Grow Old

overalls with a large wrench in her right hand. She was about to change Connor's view of how life would look with the right set of lenses in his shades. He just needed to find his way through the dark spots to navigate his way to the sweet spots in life. The world was not about things. He needed to learn how to dance through the rubble, and she was cranking up the tunes.

Floyd inspected the dent in the passenger side door of Connor's car. "Piece of cake," he said. "We'll have you out of here in an hour or two and you can forget it ever happened." He went to get his tools of the trade.

A tow truck pulled in while Connor was waiting for the repairs to be completed. Clara had disappeared to the other side of the building, and Connor was left sitting in the cramped waiting room by himself. Outside, a woman stepped down from the cab of the truck and was yelling for Floyd. Catherine is Floyd's other sister, she drives the truck and produces the fancy custom graphics that Floyd applies to the cars of his elite clientele. When Floyd did not appear in response to her yelling out his name, she came through the waiting room to see where he was. Connor looked up from the magazine he had been idly flipping through. *How odd! He had never encountered a female truck driver before. Then again, he had never met a female mechanic either.* The woman looked familiar, he looked back at the magazine. There she was, standing beside Floyd in a picture that was followed by an article praising their business. Connor read on. The McDougal Body Shop was run by a brother and sister team who specialized in custom repairs and modifications to European cars.

Irish Mist

The siblings were renowned for their excellent quality of workmanship and drew customers from as far away as Vancouver and Calgary.

Catherine came back through the waiting room, heading back to her truck after consulting with Floyd. Connor stopped her, waving the magazine in his hand. "Is this you?" he asked.

"Yes it is. We are quite proud of our accomplishments." She was about to go back out the door.

"Why is Clara not in the picture?" He wanted to know.

Catherine looked at him quizzically. Then she remembered that this man was not from around there. "Clara died. Many years ago. She was my twin sister. I guess looking at me is like looking at her." She stopped again. "Say," she said, "would you like something to eat? I have some apple pie coming out of the oven in a minute. That's why I'm in such a hurry. Would you like some? Your car is going to be at least another hour."

Connor accepted Catherine's invitation and walked through to the back of the building. He could not believe his eyes, as he stared open-mouthed at the beautiful cars waiting for their owners to collect them. All was definitely not as it had seemed at first glance. He had learned a great deal today. His hair was uncombed and his shirt hung loose, his precious car was damaged, and he was following a woman in

Chapter 3 - The Trees that Grow Old

overalls who had offered him a piece of homemade pie. He felt more alive in that moment than he had in a very long time.

Denise & Daniel

Denise has always enjoyed a walk in the woods. It looks a bit crowded today, but she knows where the tourists stop and the locals go within the park. She locks her handbag in the trunk of her car, grabs her keys, and sets off to find some peace and quiet. Daniel is sitting on a log by the trailhead, a frown on his face. When Denise comes upon him, she stops to take a sip of water from the fountain and asks the man if there is something she can help him with. Daniel looks up at her and says, "I don't think there is anything anyone can do to help me. It's a lost cause, but you are very kind to be asking." He goes back to staring at the ground.

Denise, always wanting to help, responds to his sad statement. "I'm sorry to hear that you feel that way. Are you sure there is nothing I can do to assist?" It has always surprised Denise to hear herself saying things like this. She's had no clue how to solve her own problems and simply avoided them, hoping they would disappear. The opposite was what usually happened, the small issues became larger issues and did not go away.

Daniel looks up again. "I just received some bad news. I'm having a hard time sorting things through in my head."

Irish Mist

Denise sat down on the bench. "I know what you mean," she offered. "My mother is not well. I'm having to figure out what to do about long-term care, and I don't know how to sort it out. Is your situation health related? I'm sorry if I seem nosey. You don't have to answer if you don't want to."

Daniel and Denise seemed to have a lot in common, and the conversation continued as they left the trailhead and walked through the forest together. As they shared details, some thinking-outside-the-box solutions started forming in Denise's mind. When they came back to the beginning of the trail, the two of them agreed to meet again the following week and walk the loop together.

Denise was going to do some research and see if Daniel's ideas would work for her. As she made her way back to her car, she realized that she had stopped longer than she had planned. She would have to head straight to her mother's apartment: there was no time for shopping today. She was excited to talk with her mother about some new possibilities for her care.

She pulled into her mother's driveway and let herself into the house with her own key. She found her mother still in bed. She picked up discarded clothes from the floor, encouraged her mother into a house coat, and led her through to the kitchen where she pulled out a chair at the table for her to sit on. There was a stack of unopened mail waiting to be sifted through. She would get to it while her mother was eating some lunch. After her lunch, they were going

Chapter 3 - The Trees that Grow Old

to have "the talk," something that Denise had been dreading for more than a year.

Utility bills and three editions of the local newspaper formed the pile on the formica table–nothing that required immediate attention. Denise put the envelopes that contained her mother's accounts into her own purse. She would look after those things when she got home. She took a casual look through the newspaper while her mother ate.

There it was. An advertisement for a local realtor, offering free appraisals. She noted the phone number. She moved on to the next newspaper in the pile. On the front page was a picture of new construction that was nearing completion in Port Alberni. A retirement residence. The estimate was that in six months they would be open and were currently accepting applications from eligible seniors.

A doctor's note would be required, certifying good health. She copied down the number and made a note to call her mother's doctor. At last. She had a plan. She ushered up a thank you to Daniel for his help in setting her on the path to getting her life in order. Denise took her mother's hand in her own and said, "Mom, there is something important that we need to talk about."

As it turned out, her mother had already thought about a retirement home. She had seen the promotion in the newspaper and was interested in finding out more about it. *Perhaps they played mahjong?*

Irish Mist

Denise was feeling pretty positive when she left her mother later that afternoon. She mused about the two other issues that were weighing heavily on her mind as she drove home: her husband and her daughter. She didn't even know where to start. Then she realized that she had started, just by the simple act of thinking about it. She smiled to herself and said another thank you to Daniel.

Esther & Eric

It is a beautiful day, and Esther is looking forward to her time spent with nature. She always feels better about everything when she can smell the woodsy goodness of the forest and hear the birds sing. Or just sit and listen. What she is really hoping for is to hear the wisdom of the Owl. They are one of the few that hunt during the day; she believed the term was diurnal. Either way she needed to use the bathroom first, a constant reminder of the life growing within her.

Eric watched from his aerie in the treetop as Esther left the restroom and started towards the trailhead. His keen eyes followed her as she entered the woods. Eric had been waiting for her to arrive today. It was almost as if she had called ahead and made a reservation. He was excited for her. He was excited for him. When they became one being, there would be no limits to what they could discover together. He waited impatiently for Esther to find him.

Esther was looking for her favourite spot away from the path, so she could be with the trees. She needed

Chapter 3 - The Trees that Grow Old

to be somewhere that the tourists with their clicking cameras and noisy children were not. She carefully picked her way over fallen trees and lichen-covered ground to the place she loved most. As she sat and felt the air that joins the earth with the sky wafting over her, she relaxed. She listened to the trees as they talked with each other. This was sacred to her, and Esther did not want to be disturbed. She waited for the spirits to find her.

When Eric saw that Esther had emptied her mind of the world, he flew down closer to where she sat on the fungus-decorated stump. He sent out his unique sound to her waiting ears, and as she turned her head to look at him, it happened.

It was instant. Esther could feel her heart lighten. The weight of her worry was being carried by someone else. Her sense of aloneness went with it. She stroked her belly and talked to her child. "We will be fine. The spirits of the forest will carry us where we need to go and show us what to do when we get there. This will be a journey, something destined for you and me and the people and paths we cross. Today is a new day." Esther looked up at the treetop. "We are ready."

The group of tourists who were busy snapping photos stopped their busyness to take delight in the radiant smile on the face of the pregnant woman who walked past them on her way to the restroom.

Irish Mist

Esther lived on the western outskirts of Port Alberni. She had been there for about a year and was coming to the conclusion that finding herself was not about where she was and more about who she was. She had left home under difficult circumstances and had not had much contact with her family. Suddenly, she missed her mother. Perhaps it was about becoming a mother that triggered that, but she had known that was the case for many months now. She had not talked about it the last time her mother had called to find out how she was; she had not said a word. In an instant, it became something she had to do.

As soon as she got back to the house that she shared with three other young women, she dialled the familiar 306 area code for her mother in Saskatchewan. Her family lived in a First Nations community near Regina. Her native culture had deep meaning for her, but this was the '60s, almost the '70s, and her need for change and discovery had taken her to the west coast. She did not regret her situation or the decisions that she had made, and she most definitely did not want that part of her life to end. The Owl had always given her clarity, and she did not doubt its counsel now. The phone rang and rang and eventually her older brother answered. He was rarely interested in her ramblings, less as time went on. He had no understanding of why she had left. It had only meant more responsibility for himself. He passed the phone to his mother.

Esther took a deep breath before she answered the usual question of inquiry. "Mom, I'm pregnant." Before her mother could come up with a response,

Chapter 3 - The Trees that Grow Old

Esther let her breath out with the details, ending with, "I want to come home, Mom. I need your help."

As is often the case, mothers surprise their daughters with compassion instead of chastisement. In reality, it could go either way, which is probably why some mother-daughter relationships are filled with discord. Esther's mother greeted her daughter's announcement with joy that was multilayered. The gift of a grandchild was welcomed with delight. The return of her daughter to the fold was something she had wished for. Esther's confidence that her family would help her was good to hear.

The two women kept the conversation short. Long distance calls were expensive. Esther had lots to do, and she felt a new energy moving her forward. *Saskatchewan here we come!* She placed her hand over her growing belly. *Hey, my little one, let's go exploring.*

Frances and Francis

Frannie extricated herself from the confines of her Honda hatchback. She searched for her purse amidst the pile of debris on the floor of the passenger side. She gave up and grabbed the bag of dog treats from the console between the seats and locked the door. She figured if she couldn't find her bag no one else would either. The back seat had been folded down and was piled high with what she determined were essentials for a twenty-five mile drive. It would take over a half hour to reach her therapist's office, and all sorts of things could go wrong between here and there.

Irish Mist

Frannie made her way across the parking lot, her large pockets now stuffed with dog treats. This was the best part of her week. The weekly visits to the therapist seemed to be helping her, but only in that they were appeasing her landlord's demand that she seek help for her habit of collecting things or find another place to live. She didn't think there was a problem. *There was lots of room left!* But the landlord disagreed. He was a nice man and she liked her little apartment. She could walk to the market with its sod roof, get some food for supper, or wander about the artisan shops and maybe find a trinket that she had to have. She was currently unemployed and considered unemployable because of rheumatoid arthritis. Some days, when the pain was bad, it was hard to find what to smile about. She wished she had the courage to get a dog. Until that time came around, she would continue to enjoy the dogs belonging to others and feeding them treats. People looked so happy with their pooches, so normal. Frannie thought of herself as anything but normal.

Francis is a King Charles Spaniel. He is loving and gentle, very handsome, and just a bit on the plump side. His attitude of good will and goofiness is a delight. If that isn't enough, his ability to comfort the needy is truly inspiring. He might have been a therapist in a previous life. He had been picked up by the dog pound a few weeks ago when he was found wandering around at large. Francis was now in a foster home that he shared with five other dogs. The lady that took care of these dogs-in-waiting came to the forest each day. She walked three dogs at a time, leaving the other three in her station wagon with the windows rolled down and

Chapter 3 - The Trees that Grow Old

a large bowl of fresh water until it was their turn on the trail.

Frannie spotted the group of dogs and their handler while she was still on the pavement. She had seen them before and knew the situation. She put her hand in her pocket and jiggled its contents in anticipation. "Is it all right if I give the dogs some treats? They are liver, nothing more complicated than that." She knew that it was important to address the human and get consent before she engaged in the love-fest that occurs when dogs encounter desiccated liver goodies. Ms. Foster Mom nodded her approval, and Frannie took great care to ensure that each dog was given the chance to merit the tidbit. The two larger dogs were too excited and began to fight for her attention. Francis saw this as his opportunity to shine. He sat quietly, his adorable face looking more adorable by the second, his enormous brown eyes looking like liquid pools of empathy. Frannie was smitten. She tossed aside every thought that had ever stopped her from getting another pet after her cat had died.

Ms. Foster Mom gave Frannie her business card and all the information that she would need to start the adoption process. Frannie was so excited, she could hardly wait to tell her therapist. Hopefully, her landlord would allow her to have a pet.

Frannie could barely contain her excitement. She had no explanation for the abrupt turnaround in her thinking. She manipulated her body into the driver's

Irish Mist

seat of her car and carefully put the piece of paper with Ms. Foster Mom's phone number in her wallet, which she had finally found. Her pockets were still bulging with unoffered dog treats. She would save them for Francis. As she pulled back onto the highway, she smiled. She smiled so hard that there were tears flowing down her cheeks. She was going to have someone to love and someone to love her. She would need to make some room for her new friend. Maybe not a lot of room, for he was small.

When Frannie arrived at the therapist's office, she was already contemplating suspending their relationship. He talked her out of it, because he genuinely cared about Frannie and her future. As he always did, he listened intently between the lines. As she talked about the dog and her new sense of freedom, he was happy for her, cautiously happy. He had invested more than his professional time in Frannie, and he worried that if she sorted things through, he would not be seeing her again. Finn had fallen in love with his patient. He knew that the rules were very clear, and he had not acted on his feelings, but they were very much there. He loved everything about her, and her excitement was infectious. As she chatted on about her new-found love he tried to figure out how he could also be her new-found love. He had worked his way through all the ethical considerations. He needed to find a loophole.

"Frannie, I have a few rental properties in the area of Coombs. If your landlord does not allow you to have a pet, give me a call and perhaps I can help you

Chapter 3 - The Trees that Grow Old

with that." Finn wrote his home number on his message pad and handed her the pink slip of paper with a smiley face under the number. "I really hope that this works out for you. It would be nice to have coffee together sometime, outside of the office."

Greg and Georgiane

Greg parked his grey, nondescript car in the lot close to the exit. If he had to leave in a hurry, it was a good place to be. He had to jump out of the way or be run over by some idiot in one of those expensive mid-life crisis sport cars coming in the exit, its exhaust pipes yelling, "Get out of my way!" Greg thought the man in the fancy car should be his first target. He watched and waited, but the guy wasn't moving away from his car, he was too busy checking out the babes. Greg made a mental note to check on the car when he was leaving, but for now he was moving on: there were open car windows and open purses everywhere. He spotted an older woman putting her handbag on the ground while she focused on taking a photo. It was as easy as taking candy from a baby. This was going to be a busy day.

Georgiane had dressed herself in denim shorts and a skimpy, bright red tank top that showed off her tanned skin and long legs. Her long blond hair swung loosely to her waist. She was turning the heads of men and women alike. She had a canvas backpack slung casually over one shoulder and a Kodak camera on a strap hanging between her breasts. She epitomized the avid birdwatcher, totally focused on capturing photos

Irish Mist

of a cedar waxwing or a barred owl, perhaps a bald eagle, maybe a chickadee or a wren, even a Canada goose would do. Greg spotted her a mile away—well almost.

Greg was a handsome man, but not in an obvious way. He tried to downplay anything that might help one of his victims identify him. His aim was casual, nondescript and average. But there was something about this bird-watching woman that made him want to puff out his chest and preen his feathers so that she *would* notice him. He gave his head a mental shake. *What was he thinking?* He walked towards Georgiane with caution, mostly because he was rattled by his own reaction to a potential target. He thought he would use a different approach this go-around. That is exactly the moment when Georgiane turned to face Greg. Her amazing smile caught him completely off guard. Her spirit of joy shook out any and all thoughts of pickpocketing from his mind. Poof! Gone. *What the heck?* Greg found himself stammering out comments that made him sound like a teenager. He knew he was in trouble, and this had nothing to do with petty crime.

Greg was an experienced thief. He had always been a creative lad. *Too creative*, was what his mother had always said. What came out of his mouth next, as he stood beside Georgiane, was more creative than most would have come up with any day of the week. "I'd keep that backpack of yours around your front. There are lots of dishonest people to be found in tourist loca-

Chapter 3 - The Trees that Grow Old

tions and it's busy here today. Even more opportunity for someone to pick a pocket." *What the heck was he thinking?* Georgiane smiled again and he thought for sure his knees were going to give way. He fantasized stealing her wallet just so he could return it to her and look like the hero. He had no idea what he should do, because he really couldn't think. So, instead of doing anything else, he smiled back. He stood there like a grinning idiot.

Greg had always been a bit of a misfit. He had never considered himself to be an idiot. He had thrown away any chances of within-the-law success when he had started listening to his group of friends. He skipped school to shoplift. He was good at it and earned the respect of his crowd of misfit friends. He went from shoplifting to pickpocketing. He was good at that too. Never did he need to do the nine-to-five thing like so many of those pencil-pushers that had to kiss up to a boss for a raise. If he wanted to increase his income, he simply had to seek out targets of a higher class. They weren't any smarter, just richer. He had stopped thinking about his career choice a long time ago. Maybe, if he ever got caught, he might have to reconsider. For now, though, he had gotten used to looking over his shoulder and not having any strings attached.

Yet here he was, getting emotionally involved with a target. He had been hit over the head with something, and he had not seen it coming. That was so very unlike him. He had learned to be angry. His father had taught him that. Every time he had told him that the strapping was for his own good, Greg had gotten even more angry. It fuelled his choices and it fed his need for hurting others. This, what was happening to him now, was wrong. He had to get away from this woman before she ruined everything.

Greg smiled back and walked on. He would look for another tourist who was paying no attention to the crowd. He walked further into the woods but his sense of momentum had left him. Maybe targeting the guy in the fancy car would get his anger back in gear. He went back to the parking lot, but the man had left. Greg drove out the exit and turned right, towards the east coast. He would go north from there. Lots of tourists stopped at Trent River Falls. It was a popular hiking destination and the waterfalls were spectacular.

He never got past Qualicum. The RCMP pulled him over for a broken tail light. Before he was able to hide his morning earnings, the officer had spotted the variety of wallets and several passports on the floor of the passenger seat. He now stood outside his nondescript car in his nondescript clothes, while Officer Grant read him his rights.

It had happened: he got caught. What kind of awful day was this? As he was fingerprinted and advised that his car had been towed to the pound, he wanted to blame that young woman and her amazing smile. When he sat on the cold metal bench of the cell, he wanted to blame his father. When he heard the metal bars clang shut and watched the guard walk away, he

Chapter 3 - The Trees that Grow Old

finally blamed himself. He had taken the wrong road a long time ago and he had chosen to continue on. He had told himself that the day he got caught would be the day things changed for him. Today was as good a day as any.

The mist rolled in, blanketing the eastern shore of Vancouver Island. It brought with it the emotion that comes with overturning a lifetime of bad decisions fuelled by hate. The cool breeze washed the land with fresh thoughts. Greg smiled and mentally thanked the young woman with the long blond hair.

The day was coming to a close and the sun was setting. The sky was ablaze with orange and pink as the forest prepared itself for sleep. The next group of child spirits was waiting, resting in the heart of each tree, their forever homes written on the script of tomorrow.

Irish Mist

Chapter 4
The Whistle on the Wind

The year was 1958. Newfoundland was in a difficult era, but then that always seemed the case. Despite the excitement of joining the confederation almost ten years earlier, times were harsh, especially for those who lived in the outports. Townies had it easier. Overfishing by large commercial trawlers was depleting the cod stock and tuberculosis was running rampant. The influenza had been bad enough and now this. There were rumours on the wind that a relocation program was being considered by the government. That would, in effect, close the smaller outports and offer some sort of compensation or retraining to the many fishermen and their families who moved to the larger villages. Fishermen knew no other way, what possible retraining could be of any use? Just rumours and no details, so most people spent their time speculating. The hall above the ship's chandler was getting a fair bit of use these days, with lots of talk that was turning into the folks' own version of what might be, good and bad.

Irish Mist

Gramma B had her own ideas. It was time to go. She seemed to have some sort of vision that could make sense of the past and the future. I tried to picture in my mind what that would look like, and I came up with a cartoon. Two strips of cartoon drawings running alongside each other, one of the past and one of what might come next. What could things look like for a widow and a child? Gram would figure it out, she always did. She had a sense of certainty that told her that, wherever we went, there would be food on the table and a roof over our heads. It might not be fancy, but we would have what we needed.

Gram penned a return letter to her daughter, Sybil, in Saskatchewan. Yes, she would think about her kind offer and thank you very much.

It was going to be quite the journey. I had never been anywhere else. I looked over Gram's shoulder as she made list after list. It all added up to what seemed like an impossible task, like moving a mountain.

I thought of Nathaniel, the rocks falling down on him. I thought of having to leave him behind. I thought of all the things that a nine-year-old girl could think about. I gave myself a headache. I heard the old truck pull up to the house. Uncle Cecil was here again. He was the only one of Da's brothers who came to call on us. He still had the cough and needed some more of that slippery elm powder. As Gramma B portioned out the herbs for him, she talked about my Da's house. She was asking him if he might be able to give her some travelling money in exchange for taking

Chapter 4 - The Whistle on the Wind

it over. It would give him and his family extra space that they could surely make use of, what with all the kids they had and his wife being pregnant again. Cecil said he would think about it. He left a large bag of flour by the door as payment for the medicine. Then he remembered the letter in his pocket and handed it to Gramma, apologizing for forgetting to give it to her last week. She gave him the letter for Sybil. When Uncle left, Gram put the kettle on to boil. She put away her jar of powder and looked at the letter in the airmail envelope on the table. The return address said Kenora, Ontario.

I waited around impatiently for the tea to be steeped, fiddling with a rag doll I had found that was missing a leg. At last our tea was in cups, and Gram had her brass letter opener in her hand. She still did not have any glasses to use for reading. "They cost too much," she said. She moved the letter back and forth until the proper distance from eye to print was achieved. I thought I would bust open waiting for her to start reading. "Who is it from?" I could keep my silence no longer.

"It's from your Aunt Joan. She lives in Ontario now; she used to live in Montreal. Let me read, child!" She readjusted herself in her chair. She began,

Dear Mum,

I am glad to hear that you are well. Robert and I are happy with our new home in northern Ontario. Montreal did not suit us well, and we longed to be out

Irish Mist

of the large city. Robert has secured employment as a guide in the Lake of the Woods area. He is a most excellent woodsman and fisherman. His knowledge of native plants and such has earned him a reputation with tourists and locals alike. We have built a house just outside of the town of Kenora. It is so wonderful to be away from city noises and smells and everything that makes me feel closed in. This is not Newfoundland and I cannot smell the sea, but the people are kind and the lakes are beautiful. The weather is much colder here, but the damp is not there to seep into your bones. You might like it!

I am sorry to hear the sad news of the death of Margaret and Graeme. It must be so very hard for you to be without the comfort of family. I know I have not written in a very long time, and I hope that you will forgive me my transgression. It seems there are a few of them that need forgiving. I am no longer the flighty teen that left St. John's so many years ago, and I know that you did not approve of my marriage. I hope that you will come to have a different opinion of my husband. He is a good man, kind and thoughtful. He is a true Newfoundlander; his parents still live in Placentia Bay. The eldest of his six brothers, Jim, lives here. Alan is in Montreal, Douglas lives in Regina, and Gord and Malcolm are in Calgary. It was Jim and his lovely wife, Terri-Ann, who helped us when we first got here.

We are surrounded by nature, tall trees and freshwater lakes that are jumping with fish. Sometimes, in the early dawn, the mist rises up off the water in

Chapter 4 - The Whistle on the Wind

the way that you described Ireland to us kids, an Irish mist. A mist that makes me homesick for The Rock. Some days, I long for the salt air and the whales that sing their song as they go past. But this is our life, and it is indeed beautiful. I am hopeful that you will consider coming here, at least for a visit.

Please give Robert a chance. He is not the irresponsible one. I was the irresponsible one, and I trust that we can reconcile our differences. I would very much like for Maisie to meet her young cousins, and I would very much like to meet her. I miss you, Mum. Please come.

Let me know as soon as you have made a decision, and we will help with your travel costs as best as we can.

With love always,

Joan

"What now, Gram? Will we go to Saskatchewan or will we go to Ontario? I don't know where either one of these places is, but they both sound like fun."

"We need more than fun, Maisie. We need to make proper decisions that will serve us well."

I hated it when Gram got all serious-like.

Irish Mist

Decision Time

Gram said that she wished she had money for long distance calls and reading glasses. There were other things as well, but for right now those two things were at the top of her list. I knew that I was of no help to her in making these important decisions. I wished that there was someone who could help. In that moment I realized how alone we were: shunned by relatives because of a religion that we had no belief in, shunned by villagers who thought that Gram was a witch because she used herbs. As much as I was eager and afraid all at the same time, I knew that we needed to find another home. I asked Gram about my cousins. I wanted to know about my aunt and uncle. I wanted to know if I could bring Nathaniel with us, wherever it was that Gram decided we were going.

My birthday came and went. It wasn't a spectacular event; it just moved on to the next day. Uncle Cecil came and talked with Gram a few more times, and it seemed that they had come to an accord. There were more letters that went back and forth and, finally, Gram sat me down and told me that the decision had been made. We couldn't take much with us, just the essentials that we would need for travel and her collection of medicines. I could bring my favourite doll and a few books. Nathaniel weighed heavy on my mind. I had been visiting with him every chance I got. He was all I had in the world besides my Gram. "What of Nathaniel?" I asked Gram.

Chapter 4 - The Whistle on the Wind

"Well," she said, in her measured voice, "we will just have to wait and see on that one. Perhaps Nathaniel does not want to leave. He will have to choose." That was not the answer I wanted, but I did understand why it had to be that way.

It was July before we had ourselves organized and our boxes prepared for travel. Uncle Cecil came to get us and loaded all our belongings into the back of his truck. He drove us to the ferry in Channel-Port Aux Basques and helped to make sure that we got on okay. He gave us each a hug and a tip of his cap and got back in his truck. We stood on the dock and waved as he drove away. Gram had tears in her eyes, and I had a huge lump in my throat that wouldn't be swallowed away.

The ride across to North Sydney, Nova Scotia was on rough waters, and we nibbled on dry crackers and took small sips of tea, not much else. Our bundles and boxes were then loaded on a bus that would take us to Halifax. Our boxes and bundles, that Gram was forever counting, were then unloaded and loaded again at the train station in Halifax. The crowded platform was filled with passengers: businessmen in suits holding fancy leather briefcases, salesmen with bored faces and heavy, cumbersome sample boxes resting on the ground at their feet, women in large-brimmed summer hats trying to control unruly children, and porters with carts loaded high with luggage. The train, its steam engine puffing clouds of white vapours was waiting for us to board. It was very exciting, and I

Irish Mist

was trying hard to pay attention to everything at once. This was not my little cove on the sea.

When the train leaves Halifax station it travels across the land between Canada's two oceans. The steel rails run alongside the St. Lawrence Seaway, now almost at its completion date of 1959, through the cities of Quebec and along the shore of Lake Ontario, passing through small towns until its stop in Union Station in the big city of Toronto. It veers north from there, chugging its way to the mining communities of North Bay and Sudbury, then moving westward. Thunder Bay will be the last stop before we disembark in Kenora. The train will continue west across the prairies of Manitoba and Saskatchewan. As if that isn't far enough, in Alberta the iron horse will meet the foothills of the Rocky Mountains and cross into British Columbia, where the sky kisses the sea again, on the shores of the Pacific Ocean in the city of Vancouver. Canada is a very large place.

Chapter 4 - The Whistle on the Wind

We left the potato fields of New Brunswick behind us on the first day. Gram had said something about potatoes. I tried to remember what it was. It was in an old book by Nathaniel Hawthorne she said. "Human nature will not flourish, any more than a potato, if it be planted and replanted, for too long a series of generations, in the same worn-out soil." Was she talking about us? I watched the sun set in front of us as the whistle on the wind led us like a falcon, showing us the way.

At night we shared a lovely little bed called a berth that was formed by the folded-down daytime seats. It was made up with fresh sheets and blankets and there was a large, heavy privacy curtain that pulled across the sleeping accommodations and a ladder that could be attached to the rail of the upper berth. Aunt Joan and Uncle Robert had been able to pay the extra money so that Gram did not have to climb a ladder to get into bed. I liked to peek out between the panels when people walked by. It must have looked quite comical for them to see my little head turning back and forth as they went to the loo. It was all very intricate and organized. There was a car for sitting and sleeping, and a car for eating. Large windows showed off the stands of maples and silver birch as they waved us along. There were lots of interesting people to talk with, all travellers on their way to somewhere.

I awoke as the train rumbled across the bridge onto the island of Montreal and its city in the middle of the St. Lawrence River. The train station was in the downtown core, and as we slowly pulled in I could see

Irish Mist

buildings that seemed to touch the sky. Streetcars and people and shops with electric signs and more people. I sat in my seat with my mouth hanging open like the flap on the back of a pair of long underwear. I had never seen such things. As the new crowd of passengers boarded the train, I could hear their voices. They talked funny, saying their words in a foreign tongue and all the while flapping their hands about as if words were not enough for them to be understood. There were those who spoke in English, but their sounds were strange to my ear as well—short and clipped with no melody to them. When the train moved on, its whistle signalled our departure. I was coming to like the way it filled the air.

Gram started humming to herself as the land grew large around us again and the buildings of the city were left behind. We had turned northward from the city of Toronto and its view of Lake Ontario. We had followed its freshwater shore for most of the day. There were many stops in small towns between the two cities, and the excitement of whistle blowing was wearing off.

The sound of Gram's voice became more distinct as she added words. It was a tune that I had heard before on the radio in the front room. We had left the radio behind for Uncle Cecil's family. *Would we ever be able to dance again?* This was not a dancing tune, but a thinking song, more like. I caught some of the words as she sang softly, "This land is your land, this land is my land, this land was made for you and me. As I was walking, that ribbon of highway, I saw above me…"

Chapter 4 - The Whistle on the Wind

It was another two days before the conductor walked up and down the narrow aisle, at long last calling out the stop for Kenora. My heart beat fast in my chest. We were here, far away from everything that was familiar. I held on to Gram's hand, my rag doll with its reattached leg clutched tightly to my chest. I could see a family standing on the platform. A woman who looked so very much like my mother was holding a bouquet of flowers. This place was going to be our home for many years. I did not know that then. Perhaps it is best if the future is kept as a surprise.

We stepped down onto the platform, and there they were, our family, waiting for us with smiles and flowers. Flowers. I thought Gram had stopped breathing as she dropped her large handbag and hugged my Aunt Joan. I just watched. I don't think I had ever seen her so happy. Two little girls, each with a little bundle of wildflowers clutched in their fists, stepped towards me. A tall man, with a delightful boyish grin, stood beside them, giving them a gentle nudge forward. We had arrived.

Kenora, Ontario

We introduced ourselves in a most disorganized way. There was far too much excitement to stand on ceremony with how-do-you-do's and such. I liked that. It was so much easier than the way I had been taught. Gram said that it was important to know how to do things the proper way. "Perhaps," I thought.

Irish Mist

The two little girls were six and four. Helen, the elder, was dressed in what looked to be her Sunday dress: small, embroidered purple flowers decorated her pinafore, and there were little lace ruffles around the edge of her Peter Pan collar. She had shiny brown hair and bright blue eyes. Brigid, named after our Gram, had the same hair and eyes and wore a dress identical to her sister's, two sizes smaller. Uncle Robert must have been about the same age as Uncle Cecil, and he had the same kind look about him. It was a happy look and it felt comfortable. He even spoke to me, asking me if I had enjoyed the ride on the train and what I had seen out of those big windows.

Uncle Robert didn't take long loading our belongings into the back storage area, and we crammed ourselves into the seats of their big station wagon. It was green, with wood panels running along its sides and rust eating its way through here and there. As we drove through the town, I marvelled at the size of it. Large buildings, shops, and cars and people everywhere. Never You Mind, Newfoundland, population 40, looked nothing like this. Kenora, Ontario had a population nearing 10,000. I had no idea what to think. *What would Nathaniel think?*

We passed through the centre of town and then on to its outskirts. We drove along paved roads with tree-lined sidewalks, houses side by side, set back from the road, with mowed lawns and flower beds. Still we continued on until we turned off onto a smaller road and the sidewalks disappeared as if someone had forgotten them. The trees grew thick and tall here, and the scent

Chapter 4 - The Whistle on the Wind

of sun-warmed pine filled my nose. When I thought that the forest would surely stop us from driving any farther, we turned again and slowed to a stop. Two enormous black dogs bounded out from nowhere and ran towards the car. Uncle Rob introduced them as Newf and Lad. Gram was laughing now, a wonderful, deep, belly laugh. We got out of the car like a group of giggly girls that had known each other forever. That felt good too.

He was waiting in the tree that reached above the house. I was glad to see that he had arrived safely. I had seen him when we left Halifax, sitting in a Nova Scotia pine. I had spotted him in New Brunswick when the train had stopped in Moncton. He was there again in that little town with the French name. All along our route he had kept pace with us, and now, here he was, waiting. It made my heart sing to know that he had chosen to come with us.

The house was large, built of logs and almost entirely surrounded by trees. There were two cedar-strip canoes on supports around the side of the house beside the numerous lines of neatly stacked and split wood. There was more wood in a pile to the left, with an enormous axe handle jutting out of an old stump. Beyond the house I could see a sliver of shimmering blue water. It was a warm day, warmer than I had ever felt other than when we had the cook stove in the kitchen going strong. Helen and Brigid had much that they wanted to show me and with Gram's permission I went off to play. I looked back over my shoulder as I ran off. Gram was busy counting her boxes and

Irish Mist

bundles as she stood on the front porch, and Nathaniel was watching from his perch in the tree.

The summer flew by at breakneck speed. I had so much to learn. Gram said it was a good thing that I had smarts. I learned about mosquitoes first off! Then came swimming and paddling. Ahead of me was still bicycle riding. Uncle Rob said it would be easy for me; I had good balance. I quickly grew to love him. He was always smiling and whistling a tune. Aunt Joan was the happy person I had always wanted my mother to be.

Uncle Rob's brother Jim, his wife, Terri-Ann, and their four kids lived in the next house along the road. We went back and forth, the seven of us kids, enjoying life like there was no tomorrow. I didn't quite get that—the adults said it all the time. There would always be tomorrow!

When September came around, I was enrolled in school. It had real classrooms with grades and a teacher for every grade. Gram finally got her reading glasses, and she found work for herself in the large hotel in town, where the mining company businessmen stayed. She learned to drive a car. Eventually, she convinced the owner of the hotel to let her advertise her medicinal remedies on a card stand in the hotel lobby.

Life moved forward, and we became a family. After graduating from high school I took a secretarial course. Gram was still working at the hotel, and she

Chapter 4 - The Whistle on the Wind

was able to get me a position in the office. All went well until the spring of 1968 and the night that Aunt Sybil phoned the house to talk with her sister Joan.

It was just past the supper hour when the phone rang. Aunt Sybil was more than distraught. I could hear her crying through the long distance connection. Gram took her hands out of the dishpan and dried them on her terry-cloth apron. Helen and Brigid were doing homework. They looked up from their notebooks, pencils suspended in midstroke. Aunt Joan tried to calm her sister, but by the sound of things she was getting nowhere with that. Gram came along and took the phone from her hand and spoke sharply into it. "Sybil! Get a hold of yourself. We can't help if we don't know what's wrong. Calm yourself! Go get a tissue and blow your nose." Gram always knew what to say.

When she hung up the phone 20 minutes later, we had all gathered enough information from the one-sided conversation to get the gist of it. Sybil needed an operation. She had female troubles. It needed to be done, and it needed to happen soon. She might not be able to work for months. The business that she ran from her sunroom would not survive in the hands of her husband Ray. He would surely forget to charge people for their purchases, and that would be the end of things. My guess was that we were going to Saskatchewan. I had long ago dropped the notion of travel by icebergs: it would be by Greyhound bus this time.

Irish Mist

And so it came to pass that Gram and I boarded the bus to Regina, our boxes and bundles accompanying us. I was going to stay with Uncle Rob's brother Douglas, who was an RCMP officer, and Gram would continue on to Sybil's; that was the plan. We said our goodbye-for-now to our Ontario family and took our leave from the hotel. The same lump formed in my throat as it had when I watched Uncle Cecil drive away nine years earlier. I waved to the family standing on the platform through the large window of the train. The age of the steam engine was long gone, but the sound of the whistle on the wind was the same. It parted the air ahead, like a falcon leading the way.

Esther

In the spring of 1968 Esther Dubois packed up her simple life on Vancouver Island. She said her goodbye-for-now to her housemates, her employer at the tourist centre, and the trees of the ancient forest. The father of her unborn child had moved on to a job on the north end of the island. He had never said goodbye; she hadn't either. She figured she was seven months along. She wasn't really sure and to be honest, she didn't want to know. She did know that her hippie-style top was quickly coming to the end of its ability to hide the truth. It was time to go.

She stuffed everything she could manage into a duffel bag. Her friends had given her a gift for the baby, a quilted papoose. That went into her woven shoulder bag, along with what little money she had, her personal documents, and a beaded bracelet for her

Chapter 4 - The Whistle on the Wind

mother. Esther had a ticket for the ferry to the mainland and a ticket for the train to Saskatoon. The Greyhound bus would take her from there to Regina and another bus would finally get her to the Reserve. She went out onto the #4 Highway and put out her thumb. She still had to make her way to the ferry dock.

Ben was on his return run to the courier hub in Nanaimo when he saw the young woman on the side of the road with her thumb out. He remembered the last time he had picked up a hitchhiker, and a smile lit his face as he thought about Brian. His simple act of kindness had changed his life. He slowed his truck and pulled to the side. "Where you headed?"

"The ferry terminal," she answered.

"I'm going right past. Hop in." Ben checked his mirror and pulled back out onto the highway. He wanted to ask why she was making the trip to the mainland but thought he would wait for her to say. He couldn't help but notice her pregnant state and the large duffel. She wore no wedding ring. He knew her situation could not be easy. As they passed the turn-off for the Cathedral Grove he thought about the last time he had been there and the woman who had asked him for directions.

"I'm getting the train to Saskatoon," she volunteered. "My mom lives near there on the Reserve. She's going to be a grandmother. You must have noticed. Thank you for stopping. I guess I don't look too dangerous!" She chatted on, telling him about her circumstance and her hopes for the future of her child. She laid out her feelings regarding living on the Reserve again. She did not want to be trapped into the poverty that had made her leave in the first place. Esther found the truck driver easy to talk to. There was no judgment in his attitude. Perhaps he had been a victim of judgment himself and knew what that felt like. When Ben let his passenger off at the ferry, he handed her a twenty. She would need something to eat. Saskatoon was a long way away.

Esther presented her ticket to the gate attendant and found a seat for herself by one of the many large windows. She moved her hand over her belly and talked to her child. *We're going to be okay. We have each other. Consider this to be your first official adventure. I hope there will be many more. I will protect you with my life. And when the time comes that I no longer walk this earth, I will watch you from the treetops.* The child moved within her, a sign that he had heard his mother's promise.

The ferry ride across the Strait of Georgia was a long one, and as water passed from bow to stern, Esther had time to think. It was a beautiful journey, but despite the display that Mother Earth provided for her that day, she felt discouraged. The sense of foreboding was strong and she tried to dispel it before it drowned her. Esther reminded herself that this return to the place she had fled was also a piece of her journey. She noticed the native carvings in the wood panel between the doors that led to the outside deck. As she looked for the spirit animals within its intricate lines,

Chapter 4 - The Whistle on the Wind

she thought about her own encounters with the spirits of her people: the Owl that cautions her not to be deceived by her own mind or the wiles of others, the Eagle that is her vision through challenging paths, and the Ladybug that gives lightness to her step. She felt better already. Horseshoe Bay, the mainland, could be seen in the distance.

The energy of the sun was ebbing as she put her sneaker-clad feet on the mainland. She put out her thumb again, hoping she would not have to wait long for a ride. It had been a long day, and it was not over yet. Within ten minutes, a guy in a panel van stopped for her. She suspected he was a plumber. The inside of the vehicle smelled of old pipes and the dashboard was littered with receipts and work orders. Yesterday's lunch was rolling around on the floorboards. She rested her back against the grease-stained and worn seat. Her feet were swollen and her head hurt. She was dog tired. As the plumber let her off at the station, he wished her good luck, and she thanked him for the ride. She boarded the train as the sun set behind her. "All aboard!" the conductor hollered at top volume. The train moved forward along the rails, the whistle announcing its departure with undeniable purpose to the waiting wind.

The rails followed the Yellowhead Highway and the North Thompson River through some of the finest scenery to be had in western Canada, then turned east towards Jasper and Edmonton beyond. The Rocky Mountains are more than 55 million years old and climb to an elevation of over 14,000 feet, show-

Irish Mist

ing off some of the most diverse and rugged terrain in the world. Unfortunately, the scenic beauty was lost on Esther. She put her head back and instantly was asleep. When she awoke hours later, the whistle was announcing the next stop in Jasper. After a hurried trip to the bathroom, she reached into her shoulder bag and pulled out the sandwich she had purchased while waiting for the train in Vancouver. The baby moved about in her belly, doing somersaults it seemed. She shifted her position and took a look at the man who had just boarded and was organizing his belongings. He sat down beside her. "Okay if I sit here?"

"Sure. I like company. Where are you headed? " She noticed the guitar case that he had very carefully stowed in the overhead compartment. He wasn't hard to look at either. No one was going to be looking at her for a very long time; she might as well enjoy the conversation. "I'm Esther. I'm on my way to my mom's in southern Saskatchewan. How about you?"

Dave was going to Edmonton. He was an aspiring musician in search of fame. He hoped to find it there. They talked about current music trends and the Vietnam war, protest rallies and the situation with draft dodgers. She suspected he was one of them. When Dave got off the train, Esther wished him well and got up for another trip to the bathroom. When she got back to her seat, there was another man sitting in the seat that Dave had vacated.

"Hi," she said. "I'm Esther." The man nodded and mumbled something about being tired, pulled his hat

Chapter 4 - The Whistle on the Wind

down over his eyes, and went to sleep. Esther dug into her shoulder bag for an apple and some crackers and went back to looking out the window. There was not much to see. She squeezed past the snoring passenger as best as a woman who is heavily pregnant could and went for a walk through the car and into the connecting one. The seats were arranged differently and she noticed a woman sitting by herself. "Hi. I'm Esther," she tried again. The woman hastily dabbed at her nose and Esther realized that she had been crying.

"I'm sorry," she said. "Sometimes it just comes over me and I can't stop it." Erica had travelled to Edmonton, with the hope of adopting a child and once again, things hadn't worked out for her and her husband. He was in the next car, and she had needed some alone time. Esther was speechless.

The train rumbled on across Alberta and into Saskatchewan. When the conductor called out the stop for Saskatoon, the women had come to a tentative agreement, subject to a lot more thinking on Esther's part. She hurried to the bathroom and then gathered up her things. She still had a three-hour bus ride to go before she saw Regina, and then another transfer after that.

The Greyhound bus was idling in the terminal when Esther got there. She barely had time to buy herself a sandwich before she boarded the bus and found a seat at the back where she hoped she could stretch out a bit. She was exhausted. As the bus lumbered onto the highway she fingered the charms on her woven-

Irish Mist

leather bracelet. The Owl, the Eagle, and the Ladybug. She needed to draw strength from somewhere because her own seemed to be gone. Her back ached, and her head hurt, and she second-guessed every decision she had made in the recent past. *What the heck had she been thinking? What good could come of this? How would she raise this child? What of her own life?* Esther nodded off to sleep, her uneaten sandwich in one hand and the other resting on her belly.

The bus stopped in Regina. She moved slowly towards the front but the driver called out to her that there was a route change and she could stay put. *Good thing,* she thought. *I don't know that my legs will carry me!* An older woman, struggling with boxes and odd-shaped bundles was the only passenger getting on. She chose an empty double seat near the back of the bus, and they were quickly on the road again.

Gramma B had seen the look on Esther's face as she went down the bus aisle and knew that the girl was in trouble. She wished Maisie were here to help but she had remained in Regina with Uncle Gordon. She had a job waiting for her at the Recruitment Centre. *Wouldn't be the first baby I've delivered, probably won't be the last!*

And it came to pass that Esther Dubois gave birth to a healthy baby boy in the back seat of a Greyhound bus between Regina and Back of Beyond, Saskatchewan.

Chapter 5
The Salt of the Earth

The Silver Lining

The driver of the Greyhound bus moved over to the side of the road and stopped. He leaned forward and picked up his radio handset to advise the dispatcher that he was going to be late. This was the second lady who had decided to have her baby in the back seat of his bus this month. *What was the world coming to?* He was more than thankful for the older woman who got

Irish Mist

on the bus at the terminal in Regina and had looked after things. He had been trained for emergency deliveries of babies and had done his share of it, three weeks ago in fact! But he was quite relieved that he didn't have to do it again. He was a bus driver, not a midwife! The older woman had seemed a bit odd to him when she boarded. She spoke with a thick accent that sounded very east-coast. And all that stuff she was carrying! The pregnant one, who had got on in Saskatoon and now, obviously, was no longer pregnant, had looked like every other hippie with a duffel, in search of themselves. But it was a good day. The passengers had cheered the arrival of new life, the baby seemed okay, and the old woman had things under control. He would only be a half hour late.

Brigid Byrne wrapped the newborn baby in her shawl as she gave reassurances to the young mother, whom she now knew as Esther. "Esther, my daughter lives in the next town. You need to get yourself and the little one off this bus now, or the driver will be radioing for the ambulance attendants to take you off. I doubt if you would like that. I am quite certain that you would be welcome to stay the night with us, or as long as is needed. Please consider my offer. Besides, I'm not sure how you would manage to carry a newborn and that huge duffel while you walk the mile from the bus stop to the Reserve. Sybil has a telephone. You can call your mother from her house and tell her what has happened. My son-in-law Ray is expecting me. He will be at the bus stop. Where I come from, there is always room for one or two more." Esther was too worn out to argue. She smiled at her

Chapter 5 - The Salt of the Earth

new friend and said thank you. Brigid shot a prayer arrow upwards, really hoping that what she had just promised would come to pass. She had never met Ray and had not seen her daughter in many, many years.

As the Greyhound bus pulled to a stop outside the farmers' co-op, the driver breathed a sigh of relief; the women were getting off together. Many willing hands came forward to help them get their belongings from the bus. It was an opportunity to take a peek at the new baby and offer kind words of advice and encouragement. This was rural Saskatchewan where people did that. All the time. Brigid thought she might like living in rural Saskatchewan. It was a bit like Newfoundland. The bus pulled away from the stop as a large black Chevy truck rounded the corner, with the rusted handle of an old lawnmower standing proud in its load bed, alongside—*Was that a wringer washer?* —a variety of loose tools that shifted and clanged against its sides. *This must be Ray.* Brigid put on her most endearing smile as she readied herself to meet her son-in-law. She had some explaining to do with regard to the unexpected guests.

Ray Bisbee was an easygoing barrel of a man. He didn't get upset about much: he was quick to help out and quick to laugh. He liked his work, he liked a cold beer, he had good friends, and his Sybil was a charmer *and* a good cook. Now he was meeting his mother-in-law for the first time. He hoped it wasn't a bad decision to have her come and stay for a while. He had heard some horror stories about mother-in-laws that came for a visit and never left. *Ah, whatever.* He had

Irish Mist

just hired a young fellow, name of Colb Timmons, to help out in the shop. What with Sybil feeling poorly and needing "the surgery" it was all a good idea. He was proud of his shop, Ray's Small Engine & Appliance Repair. Organization was a bit of a challenge for him, but young Colb would have that problem gone like yesterday's news.

Ray saw two women standing at the Greyhound stop out front of the co-op. The older one looked like everyone's favourite grandmother: greying hair, just the right amount of plumpness, matching hat and handbag, a circle of bundles and boxes at her feet. She appeared to be counting them. Beside her was a much younger woman, dressed in one of those hippie things, a baby in her arms, and her large duffel bag leaning against the light pole. Ray put the truck in park and went over to the women, hitching up his pants as he walked. He smoothed his hair for good measure. "Hello," he said. "You must be Mrs. Byrne. I'm Ray. Sybil had to stay back and keep track of the customers. It's a busy time of day." He extended his hand to shake hers and then thought better of it: his hand looked like it hadn't been washed in the recent past.

Brigid sized him up on the spot. There was nothing but genuine kindness emitting from this man. Now for the harder part. "Well," she smiled, "it is indeed a pleasure. Sybil has told me much about you. This young lady," she indicated to Esther, "is fallen on a difficult time. The baby came early and— Well, 'twas a good thing someone was there to help her. That bus driver wouldn't have done a lick of good. Anyways,

Chapter 5 - The Salt of the Earth

she needs a place for tonight. Can't be having her on that bus and hauling baby and duffel for miles. I'll look after her. She can share the room with me." She looked at Ray with an expression that said it was decided, and she started to pick up her things from the curb. "They's all there," she said, mostly to herself, her count complete. "And, please, call me Brigid, or Gramma B if you like."

It was a short ride to the house. Back Of Beyond was not a large place. They pulled into the circular drive that had the repair shop on one side and the back of the house across from it. A young man in mechanic's overalls waved a cheery hello and came over to help with the carrying of things. Brigid looked around at her new home-for-now. She noticed the sunroom was crowded with people as she went up the few steps to its door. Sybil looked up from the customer she was chatting with when she heard the bell attached to the frame of the porch door jingle. Esther watched as mother and daughter hugged like there was no tomorrow. She knew her own mother would never be that delighted to see her. There was that sense of foreboding again. She pushed it away.

Brigid and Esther went upstairs and settled in as best they could, fashioning a crib for the baby in a bureau drawer lined with a soft flannel blanket. One of Sybil's customers had rushed home and brought back a large box of baby things, cotton diapers, and the tiny bits that babies need. When the little one had been fed and washed and swaddled, Esther used the phone in the kitchen to call her mother. Brigid could

Irish Mist

hear what seemed to be a rather unpleasant conversation and when Esther had hung up ten minutes later, she silently left the room and went back upstairs.

Brigid gave Sybil a sideways look and followed Esther up the stairs. She found her sobbing, holding her sleeping baby. "I take it that your chat did not go well." Esther tried to get control of herself but it wasn't happening. Brigid sat down beside her and gave her a shoulder hug. "Dear child," she began, handing her a clean hankie, "I guess I shouldn't be calling you that. You're not a child anymore. Life can be very hard sometimes. Talk to me. What did your mother say that has you so upset?"

As Esther poured out her heart, Brigid realized that the baby had not been named. She had an idea, but would wait for a better time. Mrs. Dubois had been harsh with her daughter and despite her original welcoming attitude, she now wanted nothing to do with Esther or her illegitimate child. Esther had made her bed and now she could lie in it. "Well now, isn't this a fine kettle of fish!" Brigid gave her another hug, a longer one this time. Brigid left Esther to her thoughts. It looked as though she was planning to make another phone call: she had a small piece of paper napkin with a number written on it in her hand. The noise from Sybil's sunroom had gotten louder, and she went to see what the ruckus was about. She would have a pint of ale while she was at it.

Chapter 5 - The Salt of the Earth

Sybil's Sunroom

Sybil's sunroom—Brigid said it was a pub and let's not be silly about it—was packed with guests. Colb had come in from the shop, as had Ray and a host of others. Colb had shed his overalls and was now wearing a clean pair of jeans and a collared shirt. He held a brown serving tray in one hand as he cleaned off the table with a damp bar cloth, all the while chatting it up with the three ladies who had just sat down. Ray had a fresh pint of ale in his hand and was walking over to a table where two men, one older, one younger, and both skinny as sticks, looked to be waiting for his attention. Sybil had her head buried in the biggest refrigerator that Brigid had ever seen. She could hear bottles clinking about and waited until Sybil surfaced with an enormous Mason jar filled with pickled eggs. "Mum! Hi! Can I get you something?"

"I'm in need of a wee pint. Might be two by the time I'm done. It has been a long day. Don't suppose you might have any of those around here, would you?" She gave Sybil a weary smile.

"For sure, I do. Sit yourself down. I could use a break myself. But it will have to be quick, as you can see; it's a tad busy in here this evening. It'll all be over by nine o'clock. These folks are farmers and they are up with the hens!"

Brigid delighted in hearing her daughter's faint, but still there, Newfoundland brogue. "I'm here to help. I'll get me sea legs soon enough, but for now, I am

Irish Mist

all done in. And that poor girl upstairs! Her mother don't want her nor the baby. I don't know what she's going to do. So sad. Such a bright girl, just got herself into trouble like so many do."

"Perhaps she would consider adoption? You know that Ray and I tried for years to have a child, and it didn't happen. We are okay with that. We like our life the way it is. Soon as this surgery is over I will be done with the women's curse as well. Must say that won't be something that I'll miss. But there are lots of people who would love to have a child and cannot. She would be giving them a true gift. Let's face it Mum, her son will have opportunities that he would never have on a Reserve. He is neither native nor white. He will be rejected by all who think racism is an okay way of thinking. He will be loved for who he is, instead of shunned for who he is not. People pay good money for babies too! She could have a future for herself as well, go to college, get a good job. A chance for a good life for both of them."

"She hasn't named him, you know. It might make things too real for her. I had a thought. I wonder if she would consider calling him Nathaniel, you know, after Margaret's boy who died. It might give him some peace. He's still waiting for that."

Sybil heard the bell on the doorframe jingle as another man came in. "I have to get going. We'll talk later."

Chapter 5 - The Salt of the Earth

Ray had brought another round of ales to the skinny men he was sitting with, Arthur and Andy Timmons. They seemed to have something to celebrate. It showed on their smiling faces. The men clinked their bottles in a show of solidarity or something. Brigid tried to hear what they were happy about. She needed some good news. From what she could gather, Arthur, the older man, had very recently found himself in financial difficulties. The cause for celebration was that when he had gone into the post office to pick up a package, he found out that the rural mail carrier on an adjacent route had suddenly decided to retire. It was his lucky day! Cheers! Brigid always liked to hear good news. The younger man, his name was Andy, was all dreamy-eyed about a lass he had met. He went on and on about how pretty she was and her funny accent that made him smile. She had a weird name too, five names actually, but the one she used was Maisie. He had met her, just this morning, at the recruitment centre in Regina. Brigid was never one to hold back. Esther's reality would not become Maisie's if there was anything she could do about it. She turned in her chair, looked directly at the young man and said, "That would be Maisie Roisin Frances Byrne-Calder, my granddaughter. A fine lass she is indeed and your intentions had better be honourable or you will have me to answer to!" Andy almost spilled his beer.

While Brigid had been sitting in Sybil's sunroom, Esther had come downstairs and used the phone to call Erica, the woman from Winnipeg that she had met on the train.

Irish Mist

Only Some Can See

Two miles away, in the old McNab farmhouse kitchen, Colleen put down her pen and looked up from her homework at her mother. Edith fiddled with her apron ties. "You're what???" Colleen sputtered. Aunt Irene, still the ever happy ghost, swirled around her befuddled sister, barely managing to contain her laughter. Of course, Irene already knew of Edith's secret. No one could keep a secret from Irene. She had an Owl sitting on her misty shoulder. She knew all sorts of stuff that she wasn't saying anything about. Irene knew, beyond any doubt, that Arthur, despite his precarious life and procrastinating ways, was a good man, the salt of the earth, he was.

As if on cue, Arthur's truck rolled to a stop by the side door. The dogs were barking and wagging their tails, and Arthur stopped to give each of them an ear scratch. He was smiling from ear to ear and stinking of beer. He might even have done a little twirl as he came through the porch to the kitchen. Colleen was glad to see Colb get out on the driver's side and follow his father into the house. He was smiling too. Must have been a busy night in the sunroom, giving him extra tips in his pocket. He was saving up for a car, so he could take Marsha Kovetski to a movie at the drive-in.

"Art! You smell like you emptied the keg! What have you been up to?"

Chapter 5 - The Salt of the Earth

"Well, my darling, I have some very exciting news!" He grabbed Edith around the waist and gave her a slobbery kiss on her cheek. She pretended to protest but only because Colb and Colleen were watching. "I've got me a government job. At the post office." Before everyone could congratulate him, he pressed on. "And do you all realize what that means?" He paused just long enough for us to start thinking up guesses and then cut us off short. "I can get a small business loan at the bank!" He paused again. "You know what that means, don't ya?" He was really on a roll now. No one was going to interrupt. "Well it means we can start on our plans for Timmons Toddy!" He took Edith by the hand and raised her from her seat at the table, giving her a twirl in the small space that was our kitchen. When he stopped to regain his balance, Edith placed her hands gently on his chest. "Art," she said, "I have news too. I'm pregnant." Colleen's guess was that he thought better of asking, "How did *that* happen?"

Andy had followed Colb into the house. He had left his car at Sybil's for the night. As he watched the happy scene unfold, he tried to figure out how he felt about it all. He wasn't too sure how things would be with a baby in the house, or how that would affect the new family business, but everyone else seemed delighted. He was still thinking about pretty Miss Calder and her intimidating grandmother. She had surprised him with her straightforward talk, but after all, she was Sybil's mum. That explained more than a few things. He was happy with his life right now, happier than he had been in a long time, and he wanted to keep it that way. He would keep his intentions honourable in every aspect of his thinking. The meth lab was gone. He breathed a sigh of relief.

Colleen looked at her brother with curiosity. Perhaps she was not the only one with her head in the mist? She could only imagine what thoughts her brother was entertaining. *He was so weird!* Then she stopped herself. He was not so much the weird one anymore. She was actually starting to like this new Andy. The old Andy had been no fun at all.

A few days later, upstairs from Sybil's sunroom, after an almost sleepless night, Esther put her little one in the papoose that her friends had given her and went for a walk. She liked the idea of naming him Nathaniel. It was a good name. Her conversation with Erica and her husband, Tom, had gone well. Winnipeg was not that far away. There would be lots of opportunities for a better life for her son. Esther needed to think, but she knew that she had already decided. Giving Nathaniel to the couple from Winnipeg would be the best gift she could ever give to her child. This was also a gift to herself, though it certainly did not feel like it. She sought out reassurances and comfort as she walked out of town, towards the lake that was nearby. The trees would speak to her, she knew that.

It was early, and the sun was making its presence known in the sky, a ball of flame reaching upward towards the blue. The mist rose from the water, its coolness meeting the warmth of the air. Esther found a bench to sit on in a small picnic area along the shore. She emptied her mind of the world and listened.

Chapter 5 - The Salt of the Earth

Mourning doves, woodpeckers, hawks and ospreys, loons and wood ducks, the place was alive with sound. The trees whispered their wisdom through the air on currents of song. It came to her then. Her grandmother's voice. Clear and strong and warm and comforting.

Brigid found the note that Esther had left for her, saying that she had gone for a walk. Brigid needed some breakfast, and she went downstairs to see if there might be some oats in the pantry. Sybil was already dressed and in the kitchen, banging around in the pot cupboard. "I thought you might like some oatmeal. Mum. It is so good to have you here. I have missed you. Strange how life puts us together and then moves us apart." She found the pot she was looking for and poured a good portion of oats from the bag into the aluminium pot. She motioned to the freshly steeped tea in an old Brown Betty teapot with a crocheted cosy over top of it. "Mugs are in the cupboard beside you. Help yourself."

Brigid poured herself a tea and sat down at the table, pushing a pile of loose papers and things over to give herself room. She looked around at the simpleness of things. The room was larger, the windows were bigger, the appliances were newer. But, the feel of it was that of her own mother's kitchen, a lifetime ago in Ireland. "Yes, strange that. My own mother would have said that too, the piece you just said about life. Right about when I was getting on the boat that would bring me to Canada." Brigid stirred milk into her tea. "She's been gone a long time now, but I can still see

Irish Mist

her face. She was trying not to let me see her cry, as I stood with my new husband, your father, beside me and your sister Margaret growing in my belly, and we waved goodbye. I never saw her again, nor my Da. It was a hard time then. It breaks my heart to look at poor Esther having to say goodbye to her wee child. It's for the best, I suppose, but it is still hard." Brigid dug in her pocket for a hankie.

"She'll be okay," Sybil consoled. "Oh. I forgot to tell you. I got a telephone call this morning. You know the lady who brought Esther the baby things? Agnes? She called to ask how they were doing. Such a lovely woman, always trying to be of help. Anyway, her husband—I can't think of his name—works for the Department of Forestry. I had told Agnes a bit about the girl and her situation and she told her husband. When he found out that she speaks three languages and has experience as a guide, he was very excited. He wants to offer Esther a job as soon as she is able to come in and see him. How's that for good news?"

In the coming days, Esther would say goodbye-for-now to little Nathaniel. They would meet again, she knew it in her heart, and she had a legal document to make sure that it would happen. She met with Agnes' husband and did indeed get the job with the Forestry Department. She would be able to continue sharing with others her knowledge of the spirits of the earth that walk among us, seen and unseen. Brigid could see the Owl, the Eagle, and the Ladybug as they sat, ready to travel as one with her into her unlimited future. She drove Esther to the bus stop out front of

Chapter 5 - The Salt of the Earth

the farmers' co-op and watched as she boarded the bus she had just gotten off of a short time ago. Brigid did not hide her face as she cried and waved goodbye.

Back at Sybil's place, the sunroom was filling up. Ray was closing up the shop for the day and Colb, with his fresh young face and happy-go-lucky attitude would be coming inside in a few minutes to help wait on tables. Brigid found her apron from behind the kitchen door and tied it around her waist. There was something in the pocket and she fished it out. A small piece of paper with a telephone number on it. She would ask Sybil about it later. In the meantime she had a job to do, she was learning how to tend bar. This was great fun: she would have a few new tricks up her sleeve before this chapter of her life was over.

The same two skinny men as before came in and parked themselves at the same table. She remembered them as Arthur and Andy. Right. Andy was the one who was sweet on her Maisie. Agnes was there again with her two lady friends, drinking tea. There was a mixed group of sturdy-looking farmer types in the middle of the room at the longest table and a young couple off in the corner. She would keep an eye on them: there would be no hanky-panky going on as long as she was watching. She picked up her bar cloth and began wiping down the remaining tables when the bell jingled on the frame. It was a man and his wife, or so it looked. They stood there for a moment, uncertain as to what they should do. Brigid called out to them in her thick brogue. "Will yeh be having a drink? Come on over and sit yourselves down. I have a lovely table all ready for yehs." The evening passed quickly, and Brigid was pleased, when as expected, Sybil said goodnight to the last of her guests, closed the door, and turned off the lights. She had all but forgotten about the slip of paper in her pocket. "Sybil, I found this in my pocket this afternoon. Do you know what it's about?"

"There was a woman that called for you while you were taking Esther to the bus. She didn't leave a name, just asked for you to return the call." It was too late for that now. It would have to wait until morning.

Brigid trudged up the stairs to her room. It seemed empty without Esther and little Nathaniel. She thought of them sleeping in strange beds and hoped that they were not feeling as alone as she was. She looked at the scrap of paper again and wondered who might be wanting to talk with her.

She was almost too tired to even wash her face before bed. When she turned out the light ten minutes later, she could see the close-to-full moon through the window as it filled the sky with its light. She said a silent goodbye to the little boy who had sat waiting for so many years for his forever home. She was thankful that Nathaniel, the boy on the rock, could finally rest in peace.

The next morning surprised Brigid by its swift arrival. She was sure she had only just closed her eyes, and yet she could hear Sybil moving around in the kitchen downstairs. It was a grey day that smelled

Chapter 5 - The Salt of the Earth

of rain close by. Brigid took her time getting out of bed. The kitchen was empty when she got there, but the Brown Betty with its colourful cosy was filled with fresh hot tea. She took a mug from the cupboard, filled it, and sat at the table for a few moments before she cooked herself some breakfast. The old table was covered with stuff as usual, and she glanced casually at the collection of newspapers and such. She then remembered the slip of paper in her apron pocket and took it out to look at it again. There was an area code in front of the telephone number. *It must be from out of province,* she thought. She put it back in her pocket, promising herself to return the call after her oats. But before she could do that Sybil was calling her from the sunroom. "The surgery" was scheduled for tomorrow morning and there was much she still had to explain to Brigid about how things were run.

The next time she had a moment it was mid-afternoon. She could see the older couple, Claire and Walter McNab, coming in the porch door for an afternoon tea. She had tea, he had a dram of rye whiskey. Brigid thought that if she moved quickly, she could have them settled and still have time for that phone call. However, Claire wanted to chat, and her husband took the opportunity to walk over to where a group of men were standing and talking farm talk, no doubt.

Claire had been born in St. John's, Newfoundland, on a street called Hill of Chips, overlooking the harbour. She had moved to Saskatchewan a long time ago. Her husband had wanted to farm, and that is what they had done until they had retired and moved

Irish Mist

into town. Claire also had three daughters, but only one was still alive. Since there were no other guests requiring her help in the sunroom, Brigid sat down and took the opportunity to make a new friend. The two women found lots to talk about, but she still managed to keep an eye on the rest of the guests. Brigid saw that the men had helped themselves from the refrigerator. Walter had switched to beer. She hoped that they remembered to put a donation in the coffee can. Sybil had warned her about the self-service aspect of the business. Brigid returned her attention to her own conversation. The women had a right good laugh when they discovered that Claire's grandson was the same Andy that was interested in Brigid's Maisie. It felt good to spend some time with a woman close to her own age. She was liking this place more and more. She marvelled at what a small world it was, but then reminded herself that Back of Beyond, Saskatchewan, had a population of 602.

Chapter 5 - The Salt of the Earth

When she heard the telephone ringing in the kitchen, it was almost suppertime. It came as a reminder that the promise she had made to herself that morning had not been fulfilled. It had been another busy day. She answered the phone herself: *Bisbee's, Brigid Byrne speaking.* That was something she was definitely not used to doing in someone else's home. The woman identified herself as yesterday's caller. Denise was her name. She was the bearer of sad news; her mother had passed away. Her mother was Brigid's aunt from Ireland who had lived in Ucluelet, B.C. Denise would be sending a small package in the mail, something that her mother wanted Brigid to have as a keepsake. She needed a mailing address. Brigid already knew what that package would contain.

Maisie and Andy quickly became good friends, perhaps a bit more than that. There had been a bit of canoodling going on over at the drive-in. If anyone had asked Maisie what movie they had gone to see, she would have hummed and hawed, trying to remember. She loved her job. She loved Regina. She just might be *in love* as well. Gram would always be looking out for her, she knew that and it was a comforting feeling, but jeez! Giving her new friend, who just happened to be a boy, a recitation of the riot act was a bit more than she wanted. She would be 20 years old come springtime. She could look after herself.

Her Uncle Doug was an RCMP Officer. That was making things difficult enough to find some privacy. He was unmarried. Gram was a widow. They had no idea about love. Now she was going to have to deal

Irish Mist

with meeting the parents. She readied herself for a stressful evening. She put on a dress. She tidied her long, chestnut curls with a pretty ribbon that matched her dress, a touch of soft pink lipstick, and a smudge of mascara. Andy arrived at Uncle Doug's door, looking very handsome in a clean shirt and a woven tweed vest. *Yes, admit it, she was in love.*

As they drove out to the farm, Maisie was getting more nervous as the miles passed. Gram had met the original owners of the place in Sybil's sunroom and vouched that the McNabs, Andy's grandparents, were good people. Gram had also met Arthur, Andy's father. Her only criticism was that he liked his beer. Well, so did Gram: it couldn't be all that much of a fault.

When they arrived, Maisie managed to twist her ankle in a gopher hole on the way to the house. She had been distracted by the dogs, Bailey and Jack, as they rushed out to greet them. Memories of Newf and Lad surfaced. She truly did miss the dogs. She had fallen down, and there was now mud all over the side of her dress. The ribbon had come out of her hair, and her face was flaming red with embarrassment. This was not a good start. Andy, probably wanting to be a suitable suitor, lifted her off her feet and carried her through the porch area into the kitchen with her pretty pink underwear showing for all to see. Thank goodness she didn't know. He put her gently down on a kitchen chair that Edith had hastily pulled out for her. So much for first impressions.

Chapter 5 - The Salt of the Earth

Maisie looked around her at the small, plain kitchen, a hand pump beside the sink and a cook stove with a large kettle sitting on the back of it. There were cast iron pans lined up on hooks on the adjacent wall, and the place smelled like home. The scent of oatmeal and potatoes, steeped tea and difficulties, hard times and happiness filled her mind rather than her nose. It felt like her mother's kitchen, a lifetime ago. The feeling was so strong that it almost overwhelmed her. And then she spotted Irene. She knew that Irene was like Nathaniel. She had no idea how she knew, but she did. Irene knew as well. She swirled around Colleen and wrapped herself around Edith in a protective hug.

Maisie didn't quite know what to say. She managed to make reference to her grandmother having met Andy's grandmother and how delighted she was to meet Andy's family. That was what was coming out of her mouth, whereas her mind was spinning a different thought: *my mother talked to walls, my grandmother listened to owls, and I saw a little boy who wasn't there. Now, I can add another to the list!*

Maisie and Colleen hit it off instantly. It seems they had a few things in common, one of them being the ability to see Aunt Irene. She fell in love with the whole family, even the socially distant Arthur. As they sat around the old harvest table, Maisie felt like she had found a new home. They passed the potatoes and crossed arms over the salt cellar and they shared stories of adventures from the past. Andy drove Maisie back to town. She was going to stay with her Gram for the night. As they sat parked in the circular gravel drive between the house and Ray's shop, they talked about a future together. Any hanky-panky that might have happened was abruptly stopped in its tracks by the lights of the sunroom coming on. Maisie said a quick goodnight to her new friend, who happened to be a boy, and went inside.

The package didn't arrive from British Columbia for another week. Colb brought it into the house when he was done in the shop for the day. He had been in to see Marsha Kovetski on his lunch break and had run out of time to deliver it earlier. It was as Brigid had expected. An intricate silver charm. The Owl. Her aunt had been blessed with the gift of sight from her mother, and now Brigid would pass the charm to her granddaughter Maisie. It was how it was supposed to be. It could not be earned or learned. It only came as a gift, passed down from the Irish Healers of long-ago generations.

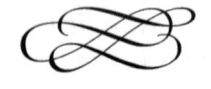

Epilogue

Irish Mist

On a Saturday morning, Colleen sat on a small mound of grass, not far from the well. She was thinking. She had a lot of things going through her mind, and she was trying to sort them into piles. It was easier that way. The dogs were wandering about, sniffing as dogs do, and peeing on the particularly interesting bits. She would like to be able to do that, just pee on something and then walk away without another thought.

She had a library book beside her. It was about Africa. The new teacher in town had encouraged his students to study geography and learn about things outside of their own country. He had told them, "There is a whole world out there, places that look different, and people that live different." She thought it was a bad idea to correct his grammar. She knew about those things. But she didn't know about Africa, and so she would read about it. It was a storybook, with lots of pictures of children with dark skin like the new teacher, Mr. Hassam. None of the students had ever seen a person who looked different in that way. Colleen liked the melody of his voice and the rich brown tone of his smooth skin. Mr. Hassam was a kind man, and he had a wonderful way of thinking that made her want to think more. She hoped he would make Back of Beyond, Saskatchewan, his home.

She focused her attention back to her book. She was reading a chapter on Kenya. It told the story of a mother who warned her child to never walk under a tree at night: there were spirits who lived in the trees. Colleen thought that was very interesting, she wished to write a book someday, a book about spirits who lived in odd places.

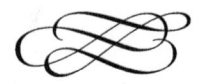

About the Author

Kris J. Rennie was born in Montreal, Quebec. She is a Cape Bretoner by descent. She has, just recently, found her birth family. But that is another story.

Always wanting to explore and experience what life has to offer and ever at the ready for a road trip, Kris and her husband, Rob, have been across the United States and Canada, coast to coast and beyond, seeking out and soaking in the local folklore. East coast lobster and west coast salmon, fresh off the boats, a local pub and a wee pint are always something on their travel agenda.

"She's a People Watcher, that one," could be said of her.

Kris began her writing career in a Montreal High School, composing credible excuse notes for absenteeism in exchange for coffee and what were then called "Fried Butterflies" at the local diner. She never really stopped after that, and she still writes creative reminder notes for her husband and seven grandchildren. She has no more excuse notes to write, so here she is— no excuses.

Pacific Ocean

Yukon

Northwest Territories

Nunavut

British Columbia

Alberta

Manitoba

Vancouver Island

Jasper

Edmonton

Saskatoon

Back of Beyond

Regina

Winnipeg

Ken

Saskatchewan

Map of Eastern Canada

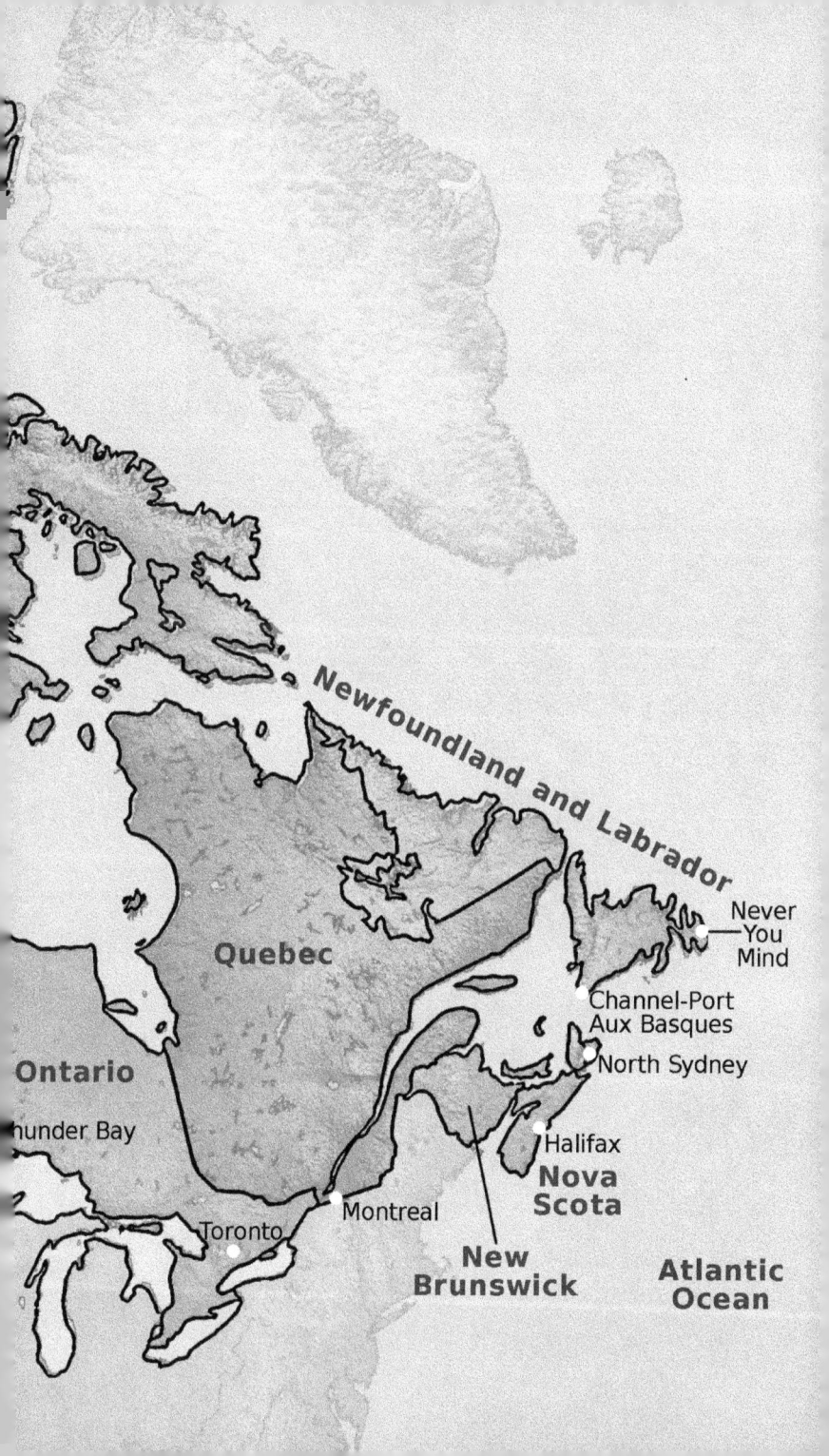

- Thunder Bay
- Ontario
- Quebec
- Toronto
- Montreal
- New Brunswick
- Halifax
- Nova Scota
- North Sydney
- Channel-Port Aux Basques
- Newfoundland and Labrador
- Never You Mind
- Atlantic Ocean

CPSIA information can be obtained
at www.ICGtesting.com
Printed in the USA
BVHW090207190920
589010BV00004B/14